THIS WAY HOME

Also by Wes Moore

Discovering Wes Moore

Also by Shawn Goodman

Something Like Hope
Kindness for Weakness

THIS WAY HOME

WES MOORE
WITH SHAWN GOODMAN

Delacorte Press

Text copyright © 2015 by Wes Moore
Jacket photograph © 2014 by Getty Images

All rights reserved. Published in the United States by Delacorte Press, an imprint of Random House Children's Books, a division of Penguin Random House LLC, New York.

Delacorte Press is a registered trademark and the colophon is a trademark of Penguin Random House LLC.

randomhouseteens.com

Educators and librarians, for a variety of teaching tools, visit us at RHTeachersLibrarians.com

Library of Congress Cataloging-in-Publication Data
Moore, Wes.
   This way home / Wes Moore with Shawn Goodman.—First edition.
         pages cm
   Summary: Elijah, seventeen, has always been sure of just one thing—basketball—and believes it will be his way out of West Baltimore, but when gang violence knocks him down, helping a veteran repair his rickety home helps Elijah see what really matters.
   ISBN 978-0-385-74169-9 (hc)—ISBN 978-0-375-99019-9 (glb)—ISBN 978-0-375-98671-0 (ebook)
   [1. Basketball—Fiction. 2. Gangs—Fiction. 3. Best friends—Fiction. 4. Friendship—Fiction. 5. Conduct of life—Fiction. 6. Veterans—Fiction. 7. African Americans—Fiction. 8. Baltimore (Md.)—Fiction.] I. Goodman, Shawn. II. Title.
   PZ7.1.M668Thi 2015
   [Fic]—dc23

                                                                    2014032608

The text of this book is set in 11-point Baskerville.
Jacket design by Ray Shappell
Interior design by Patrice Sheridan

Printed in the United States of America
10 9 8 7 6 5 4 3 2 1
First Edition

To James, my soul. I am always here,
next to you, rooting for you.
—W.M.

Maryland Public Secondary Schools State Championship: Fourth Quarter

ELIJAH STOOD TALL at the top of the key, thinking, watching, waiting for something to happen. The other team had played a nearly perfect game, but several players were beginning to tire and show weakness. A point guard lagged half a step behind, breathing through his mouth, sucking in air in desperate gasps. And the power forward, the one with shoulders as broad as a house, slouched like a tired kid at the end of a long day.

"Now," said Coach Walters in his big, final-seconds voice. "Do it now."

But Elijah would not be rushed. There was time, and he knew what to do. He dribbled slowly, languidly, until he made eye contact with Michael, the center, who was also one of his oldest and closest friends. Michael responded immediately, stomping his tree-trunk legs on the varnished maple planks, two hundred and fifty pounds screeching to a halt and obliterating his opponent's momentum in a perfect, albeit somewhat violent, pick.

Elijah's coach paced the sidelines, booming instructions over the noise of the crowd. Something about running the number-three offense, which would put Elijah in the middle of the lane and likely draw double or even triple coverage. No, his team didn't need number three. They needed to get the ball into the hands of

Dylan, a hyperkinetic wisp of a kid who could cram three or four moves into the time it took other players, even really good players, to bring off one. Dylan, Elijah's other best friend, who could pull the most difficult pass out of thin air with his skinny rubber-band arms and legs.

Elijah passed the ball and made his move toward the goal.

One step.

Two steps.

He turned his head in time to see Dylan pluck the ball from the air. The skinny boy brought it down and hooked it around his back, a beauty of a pass that was crisp and perfectly timed. Elijah received it midstride and felt his whole body set free, spinning and gliding around players, all rhythm and balance and movement as he made his inexorable way toward the hoop. He launched off his right foot into the air, arm outstretched. Body climbing. The ball practically glued to his palm, ready to be slammed home in an epic final play. . . .

Elijah's teammates lifted him off his feet.

"How's it feel to be state champs?" yelled one of them.

"Not as good as I thought it would," said Elijah, even though he knew it was not the correct thing to say. Winning State had been his team's goal for three years, and you were supposed to be happy when you reached your goal. Actually, you were supposed to go wild and jump on each other and say things like "I can't believe it. This is the best day of my life."

You weren't supposed to say what he'd said.

But the noise in the gym blasted hard off the walls and the floor, leaving little chance of his words reaching anyone. Instead, the waves of his teammates' excitement rolled over Elijah. Shouts, bear hugs, and affectionate slaps on the back. He continued to force a smile and allowed himself one last chance to scan the bleachers for the man in the photo he kept under his bed—his father, who, predictably, had not come to watch him play.

Why would you even think he would?

Coach Walters pulled Elijah away from the rest of the team. His expression was unreadable. "We need to talk."

"I know," said Elijah. "I should have run the play you called for. I'm sorry."

"You're sorry?" Coach Walters laughed. "You did exactly the right thing. I'm proud to be your coach, even if what you're doing out there to win isn't coming from me."

Elijah started to explain, but his coach held up a hand. "We need to talk about college. Finding the right school and getting you on their radar for a scholarship."

"I've gotten a few letters," said Elijah.

"Well, after tonight you're going to be getting a lot more." Coach Walters put a hand on Elijah's shoulder. "Now go over there and give your mother a hug. Celebrate with your teammates. We'll talk tomorrow; I've got a couple of ideas."

But Elijah was already formulating his own idea. He knew his father was still out there somewhere. Maybe far away, in a different state. Maybe he hadn't even heard that his son was going to play in the state championship. But if there were a bigger tournament, something so big and famous that it would be televised nationally, like on ESPN, and Elijah's team made it to the finals . . . he would come.

1

FROM THE VANTAGE point of an old, splintered bench, Elijah focused his attention on the far court action, which was looking radically different from the safe, organized competition of his high school games. A meaty guy with prison tattoos carried the ball like a battering ram to the hoop. Elijah winced as the guy plowed over a kid from the opposing team and nearly knocked him out of his Jordans. The kid groaned as he wiped at his bloody knees; of course, no one called a foul.

"Hey," said Dylan, who was dressed in ridiculously oversized shorts and a T-shirt.

"Hey yourself," said Elijah, his eyes still fixed on the game. The guy with the tats had just dunked over the head of the other team's equally beefy center.

"Damn," said Dylan. "Is that guy playing in Hoops?"

"Yep," said Elijah. "And you're going to be guarding him."

"He looks like he just got out of prison," said Dylan. "And you know what he was in for?"

"Tell me," said Elijah.

"For killing the last skinny white boy who was stupid enough to guard him. Not everyone's like you, you know."

"Meaning?" said Elijah.

"Meaning I'm not six-four and carved out of steel. I don't wanna be that dude's next parole violation. No way."

Elijah laughed and held a fake microphone in front of his friend's face. "Strong words, Dylan. Anything else you'd like to say to your fans out there before you and your teammates become the first seventeen-year-olds to win the adult division of the biggest three-on-three tournament in the state?"

Dylan grabbed the imaginary mike and tapped it. "Is this thing on? Okay. I'm saying I just want to play ball and be a lover. You know what I mean? That's my message to the young people of the world. That's what I want to be known for, basketball and . . ."

"Sexual potency?" offered Elijah, returning the invisible microphone to his friend.

"Exactly. What you said."

Elijah threw an arm around the smaller boy's shoulders. "If that guy *does* kill you, make sure to draw the foul, okay? Coach Walters says we've got a real chance, but every point has got to count."

Dylan squirmed out from under Elijah's arm and tried, unsuccessfully, to get his bigger, stronger friend into a headlock. Eventually they settled down to resume watching the game.

"But seriously," said Elijah. "What do you think about these guys? In case we do end up playing them."

"That dude over there's got no left," said Dylan.

"And that one?" Elijah pointed at the guy with the prison tattoos, who had abandoned the game in favor of shoving one of his opponents. "Your ex-con friend."

"Ha!" said Dylan. "He's got a bad temper. Guys like him lose their focus when they get frustrated."

"Then tell me how you're going to frustrate him in the tournament."

"I'm not," said Dylan. "I'm gonna be home sick, watching you guys play on TV." He coughed for effect. "I feel a cold coming on."

Elijah shook his head. "You're going to be right here doing your thing and getting inside his head with those fast, skinny legs and crazy dribbling skills. You're going to make him run with you, which, of course, he can't because he's too big and stupid and bulked up. And then all we have to do is sit back and watch him self-destruct."

"Whatever." But Dylan smiled, because he understood. He got up off the bench and grabbed his ball. Then his pale, thin legs scissored expertly while he dribbled quick and low between them, the ball caroming off an invisible midpoint at exactly the right moment.

"That's right," said Elijah appreciatively. "You're like a hyperactive metronome. Be the metronome."

"The what?" said Dylan, not missing a beat with his dribbling.

"Never mind." Elijah lunged low, but Dylan carried the ball a fraction of a second longer than usual and then pivoted away. He moved with uncanny speed onto an empty court, where they began their unique interpretation of practice, which consisted of endless variations of passing drills and set plays, and three dozen suicide sprints. When they finally stopped, sweat-soaked and exhausted, the sky had changed from dusk to full-on dark; everyone else had gone home.

Dylan pointed toward his mother's car. "You want a ride? My moms said she'll take us to McDonald's for milk shakes."

"No, thanks," said Elijah. "I'm going to get a run in."

"Why?" Dylan stuffed his ball into his duffel bag.

"Got to get strong," said Elijah.

"But you're already strong," said Dylan. "I mean, not as strong as me, but you know . . ."

Elijah nodded, holding his fist out for a bump. "Thank your mother for me."

Once he was alone, he shook out his legs and then leaned against the chain-link fence to stretch. His calves and quads were sore, but the good kind of sore, the kind that meant he'd worked hard and pushed himself. The kind that meant he *was* getting stronger. He scanned the parking lot, which was empty except for a lone figure, arms crossed over his chest as he stood next to a black Mercedes with gleaming, oversized rims. The guy wore a dark hoodie that hid his face.

Elijah shouldered his pack and started jogging, past the overflowing trash cans and broken playground equipment. Past the padlocked bathrooms, and bicycle racks shackled with rusted, cannibalized frames, their seats and wheels and derailleurs long since stripped away and sold. He tried not to look back at the car but couldn't help it; the figure was still there staring intently. Now nodding to him. So who the hell was he? A mysterious ballplayer with a nice car and nowhere to go? A drug dealer? Gang recruiter?

Something worked loose from Elijah's memory, a piece of a conversation he'd overheard in school about a new gang that was trying to out-murder the other gangs. He hadn't paid attention at the time because he lived where the neighborhoods were still safe and good, just east of the park known as the Battlegrounds. But now he wished he could remember something useful about what he'd overheard, at least the gang's name. What did they call themselves? Blood something. Blood Street Nation, that was it. *Christ,* he thought. *Some name.*

Elijah returned the nod and then broke into a loose, easy stride in the direction of his home. He didn't look back again.

2

THE RUN HOME from the Battlegrounds was one of Elijah's secret pleasures. He wouldn't have admitted it, but the freshly painted houses and well-tended lawns made him feel inexplicably happy. He loved the big inviting porches with wicker furniture, and toys scattered everywhere: yellow plastic Wiffle bats, skateboards, and toy guns. And the trees, some of which were a hundred years old, anchored by strong, invisible roots. It was like his neighborhood had wrapped itself around its families, promising a lifetime of good things, like backyard barbecues and graduation parties.

Elijah knew it wasn't as perfect as it seemed; if you scratched the surface, you'd find plenty of bad things. Alcoholic parents. Money problems. Divorce. The same as anywhere else. But it still felt good to jog by and see real families: mothers pushing strollers or weeding flower gardens, fathers tossing footballs with their sons or washing their shiny new cars. He tried to extract similar scenes from his own past, but there were none; his father had left when he was two years old, and try as he might, he couldn't remember the sound of the man's voice or even what he looked like. As for a new car, they had enough money for rent and bills but not much else.

"I'd rather live in a nice neighborhood and take the bus than live someplace dangerous and have a car," his mother always said.

Elijah quickened his pace, focusing on his breathing, his fast-moving, elongated shadow keeping pace with the beat of his heart. He wished he could remember just one thing about his father, a favorite shirt or the kind of aftershave he'd worn. Or, better yet, the feeling of his small boy's hand held by his father's, which he imagined as larger, callused from work, but gentle, too. But he remembered nothing, and slowly, the bitterness found its way in and threatened to overtake him. Because his father's absence was as real and unyielding as the pavement under his feet, and it never stopped hurting. He gained even more speed, trying desperately not to care.

ELIJAH BROKE HIS stride on Grider Street as the red-and-blue strobes of a police cruiser flashed across his T-shirt. A loose crowd gathered around a perimeter of yellow crime-scene tape: young couples with baby strollers; a cluster of old men wearing snap brim caps and feathered fedoras; teenage girls snapping pictures with fake-jewel-encrusted cell phones; and, finally, a group of women, one of whom clutched a fist of balled-up tissues to her face, her makeup running in lurid streaks.

"No," the woman with the tissues said. "No, no, no."

"What's going on?" said Elijah to a boy he'd played ball with a few times. Darren something.

Darren waved him over and made room behind his section of yellow tape. He pointed at a body in the middle of the street. "You know who that is?"

Elijah craned his head to see around one of the big white police cruisers. Behind it, he caught a glimpse of a leg, and a single Adidas Superstar sneaker, the laces and Velcro strap purposefully undone. Rivulets of dark liquid—too dark to be blood, but he knew that was exactly what it was—collected in a small pothole, glistening.

"No. Who is it?" said Elijah.

"Ray Shiver," said Darren. "You know. That smart kid."

Elijah stared, not believing. Ray Shiver, who lived not four blocks away—closer to the Battlegrounds than his own house, but still on the *right* side—was a good kid. He got straight As and played in the jazz band at school assemblies. "What happened?"

"Gang related," said Darren, as though that explained everything—the ambulances and police cars, the crying women, and, of course, the body. "At least that's what I'm hearing. I saw a big hole in his back when they rolled him over. They must have shot him with a forty-five."

Elijah had no idea how Darren knew this, but he decided not to ask; questions like that often led to unwanted answers, answers that might change how he viewed their neighborhood. And he liked his home. It was safe, and good.

The woman with the tissues pulled herself free from the other women and made a run toward the plastic tape, letting loose a slow, terrible scream.

"Oh, look out!" Darren shoved Elijah out of the way.

The woman hit the tape, and it stretched and wrapped around her thick waist. One of her heels snapped off on the curb, and she went down, howling with grief.

Elijah turned his back on the scene and sprinted the rest of the way home.

3

"IT'S PAST NINE," said his mother before he could unlace his worn-out Adidas kicks. "Where have you been? How come you didn't call?"

"I'm sorry, Mom. I forgot. I was practicing." Elijah knew he should have told her about the shooting, but it didn't seem real yet. In his seventeen years he'd never seen a dead person, much less a murdered kid; he didn't know how to make sense of it. Better to wait and let her find out on the eleven o'clock news.

"Practicing writing your research papers, I hope." She turned her back and walked into the kitchen, where a casserole dish rested on the stovetop.

"I finished English and econ already. I'll work on history after I eat."

"Mm-hmm." She heaped his plate with baked mac and cheese, and then prepared a much smaller plate for herself. "You were playing basketball?"

"We've got the tournament in two weeks. Coach Walters, from school, said he was going to call a college scout who might come see me play." Elijah pulled up a stool at the Formica island that functioned as a countertop, kitchen table, and desk at which to do homework and pay bills.

11

"Anything connected with college is good. But does that mean Dylan and Michael were with you, helping you *not* write papers?"

"Dylan was with me. Michael's so full of himself these days, he says being himself is all the practice he needs."

"Funny. That boy's always been his own biggest fan. Even when he was five years old." She allowed a brief smile before returning to the business at hand. "Speaking of Dylan, I had a cup of coffee with his mother after church."

"And?" Elijah pushed the food around on his plate, wondering how he could get out of eating without offering an explanation for his lack of appetite. *Sorry, Mom, but I saw a dead kid on the way home. He had a hole in his back. Maybe I'll eat later.* Tentatively he took a bite; his stomach churned but accepted it, and he took another.

"She's worried about him."

"Why? What's wrong with Dylan? I just saw him; he's fine."

His mother frowned. "You know he's falling behind in school. She says he might not graduate on time."

"He'll be fine," said Elijah. "I helped him finish his English portfolio. That's his worst class. And he's going to double up next year on gym and tech. That'll get him the credits he needs."

"She's worried he'll turn out like his brother, who's in prison. Or worse, his father, who used to be in prison."

"Dylan loves his father," said Elijah. "I've met him; he's not so bad. He looks a little rough, but he took us once to the batting cages and to ride the go-karts. And he bought Dylan a gold chain with a basketball pendant for his birthday. Dylan wears it every day."

"Mm-hmm. It's awfully easy for a man like that to come by once in a blue moon and do the fun things. What's hard is sticking around."

When he'd finished eating, Elijah stood and wrapped his arms around his mother. The top of her head barely reached his chin.

"Go get your homework done," she said. "And then you can

tell me about this big tournament. Maybe I'll take off from work and come watch you play."

IT WAS AFTER midnight when Elijah put the finishing touches on his research paper. He cleaned his sneakers with a washcloth and dish soap; they were in hopeless condition—scuffed, and worn through the toe—but there was no way of getting a new pair before the tournament. He'd have to make do.

Eventually he lay awake in his bed thinking about Ray Shiver's body, laid out in the middle of Grider Street. And Ray's mother, tangled in yellow police tape, wailing like it was the end of the world. He wondered if Ray had a father, and where he'd been. Working? Missing in action?

Why did it always come back to fathers? Probably because of how badly he wanted his to materialize and take him to ride go-karts or to buy him a gold chain with a basketball pendant on it. It didn't have to be about gifts and fun things, either; he'd be content for them to sit and talk, or run errands together. Anything. Even if it weren't permanent and, like Dylan's and Michael's fathers, he came and went according to his own rhythms. The important thing would be that they would hang out and get to know each other. And Elijah could say in casual conversation, at school or with his friends, *My father this*, and *My father that*. Instead of always saying nothing.

But none of that mattered, because this time he had a plan.

He closed his eyes and imagined the scene: stepping onto court number one at the Battlegrounds, in front of hundreds of spectators. Crowds would be lining the fences, little kids sitting on bigger kids' shoulders to see the action. And Elijah would look out and know that his father was there. Even though they hadn't seen each other in fifteen years and six months, Elijah would pick his father's face out of the crowd. Because he was his father, and

Elijah his son. And that relationship, that fact, didn't change, even in the face of time and distance.

Elijah pictured his father raising his fist in the air at key moments in the game, cheering and saying things like, *Did you see that? That's my son out there. Elijah Thomas.*

And as he drifted off to sleep, he imagined his favorite part, what they would say to each other after the game.

> **His father:** "I'm sorry, Elijah. Leaving was the worst mistake of my life. I've thought about you every single day."
>
> **Elijah:** "Then why did you go?"
>
> **His father:** "Because I was stupid. Because I didn't understand. . . ."
>
> **Elijah:** "Why come back now?"

No, it wouldn't be like that at all, because Elijah wasn't interested in the back-at-you stuff that played out on TV shows. He wanted to get to know his father. And so it was fitting that, in the end, they would each say the same thing. Something simple and true.

"I've missed you."

4

"OVER HERE." Michael waved a thick hand from their table in the crowded cafeteria on the last day of school. His hair was perfectly trimmed, and his round, chubby face sported a narrow line of beard and mustache.

"Next time we come here, we'll be seniors. Do you believe that?" Elijah sat down with his tray, which contained a regular school lunch plus three cartons of milk, a banana, and two apples. He let his heavy pack slide off his shoulders and thump onto the floor.

"I'm ready to be graduated," said Michael. "Damn, you eat a lot, and what are you carrying, books?"

"That's right," said Elijah. "Something you wouldn't know about."

"I read books; I just wouldn't be caught dead carrying them."

"Why not?" Elijah knew he was playing into one of his friend's ridiculous setups, but he didn't mind. Next to basketball, goofing on each other was a favorite pastime, and he was happy to play the role of straight man.

"Because it's all cool for a while, being literate and stuff. But then you wake up one day wearing penny loafers and a cardigan sweater, working as an office assistant or something. Come home

15

to eat frozen Swanson dinners with your fat, no-sex-having wife, and watch *Dancing with the Stars* together."

"You're crazy." Elijah shoveled his food while keeping one eye on the clock; even on the last day of school, he wasn't going to be late for class.

"I'm serious, man. It happened to my uncle Cole. Dude used to be *hard*—ripped with muscles, drove one of them new Dodge Challengers. Nobody messed with him. But then he started reading all these books like *Freakonomics,* and *Blink,* and *Outliers,* and next thing he's drinking soy lattes at Starbucks and living in a condo with Ikea furniture and matching towels. Brother went soft."

"Speaking of soft." Elijah poked his friend's belly, which was straining the buttons of his pressed Hilfiger oxford. "When are you going to get in shape? Hoops starts in nine days. We need you fit, not fat."

"Don't worry. I got a little something for the team that's going to make us all run like gazelles."

"Team T-shirts?" said Elijah.

"Way better. You'll see. Meet me at my locker after school, and bring Dylan."

ELIJAH FOUND DYLAN in the library with a stack of X-Men comics. "Come on, man. We've got to meet Michael."

"I'm almost done," said Dylan, flipping the pages as fast as he could follow the pictures. "Wolverine's about to mess this dude up."

"Who, Sabretooth? He can't beat him."

"Wolverine's got Adamantium claws. He can beat anyone. Check it out!"

Elijah grabbed the comic out of his friend's hand and headed for the librarian's desk. "Bring it with you."

"Can't." Dylan tagged along behind him. "I owe late fees. Again."

"How much?"

"I don't know. A lot. Like, way more than the stuff is probably worth. But you don't owe anything, right? You can check it out for me."

Elijah sighed and pulled out his card. "Are you going to turn it in on time?"

"There is no *on time*," said Dylan. "We get to keep it all summer. What are you, anyway? Some kind of library RoboCop who beats late fees out of villains who read too slow?"

"Exactly."

They walked to the end of the main hallway and waited at Michael's locker, faces buried in the comic.

"What's up?" Michael flashed his trademark corner-of-the-mouth grin. "I'll be seriously disappointed if that's not a dirty magazine. Tell me you two ain't reading comic books."

"What's wrong with comics?" asked Dylan.

"Do I really have to tell you?" said Michael.

Elijah held up the cover, which featured an inked cartoon beauty. "It's not *Penthouse,* but the Scarlet Witch is hot. Admit it."

"No way," said Dylan. "That's Magneto's daughter. Even her beauty is an illusion. She can't be trusted."

"*You* can't be trusted, because you're too damn simple." Michael shook his head and spun the tumbler on his locker. "Check out what I scored for you two nerd boys. And remember, the proper show of gratitude is to bow down and address me by my proper title—King Michael. Or Your Majesty."

Inside were three orange Nike boxes.

"Whoa." Dylan's eyes went wide with the promise of a better future, one that began with a pair of new sneakers.

"Are those . . . ," said Elijah.

Slowly, solemnly, Michael lifted the lid of one of the boxes and peeled back the tissue paper. The most beautiful pair of four-hundred-dollar shoes any of them had ever seen lay before them. A collective sigh of appreciation escaped from the boys as they took in the orange and white swirled mesh, the ubiquitous green swoosh, and, of course, Kobe Bryant's scrolling signature.

"You got us Kobe 10s?" said Dylan, just one unit of happiness away from an aneurism.

"Houston colors, too," said Elijah. "I'm giving you a new title: the Grand High Exalted Mystic Ruler of Street Ball. Your name will be spoken in reverent tones from here to the Battlegrounds."

"I like that," said Michael, handing the boxes over. "Maybe books ain't so bad."

"How did you . . . ," said Dylan, unable to form the rest of the question.

"Never mind the how." Michael opened his own box. Size fourteen. "We're playing in the adult bracket this year, so we got to have our act together. No more broke kicks, and no more tripping on our faces because of a damn footwear malfunction. We're gonna stand proud this year, and people are gonna say, 'Who's that? Michael? Elijah? Dylan? Those ain't high school kids. They're men.'"

"So, what do we have to do to keep 'em?" asked Dylan.

Michael laughed.

"Seriously." A worried look spread over Dylan's face. "You know how my mother is. She heard about Ray Shiver and doesn't want to let me out of the house. So if I've got to do anything . . ."

"Relax," said Michael. "How long you known me?"

"Too long," said Dylan.

"You got that right, but you don't have to do nothing except kick butt on the court. I'm not setting you two up for nothing shady. Now, what do you think?"

"I think you're like black Santa and that giant pink rabbit

all rolled into one, because this is like Christmas and . . ." Dylan stared off blankly, searching for the word.

"And Easter?" added Elijah.

"Yeah," said Dylan. "Anyway, these are awesome. I think I might give you a hug, Michael. Can I give you a hug?" He moved in slowly, arms spread wide.

"Man, get off me," said Michael.

"Seriously," said Elijah. "Where'd you get them?"

"Where shoes come from—the shoe store," said Michael. "What's it matter?"

"I've been dreaming about having a pair of Kobes for a long time," said Elijah. "But my mom is the same way as Dylan's. . . ."

"You two need to relax." Michael put the lid back on his own box. "I found us a sponsor, all right?"

"A sponsor. Who?"

"Someone who recognizes our talent."

Elijah held Michael's stare.

"You don't know him. He keeps a low profile." Michael added, "He's got mad money."

"Like how much?" said Dylan. "You think he'd get us jerseys and shorts, too?"

"Maybe, but you know what?" Michael slammed his locker shut. "If Elijah's all suspicious, I'll give 'em back. We can wear our old busted-up kicks."

"Wait!" Dylan gripped his orange box to his chest. "Elijah, come on. He says it's all good."

Michael saluted, and held up his right hand.

"You swear?" Elijah touched one of the sneakers, running his finger gently over the mesh toe box. He looked down at his current shoes and wiggled a dusty sock through one of the many holes.

"Man, I swear to the Patron Saint of Expensive Footwear." Michael waited for the silence that meant acceptance. "You *know* you want to try 'em on and play."

AFTER A ROUGH and fast-paced pickup game at the Battlegrounds, the boys stopped under the shade of a live oak tree to listen to Jones, the ever-present courtside bookie who entertained the sidelines with his endless and fast-moving stream of bullshit. Jones was almost as well known for his fashion, which today consisted of a red Kangol hat, cutoffs with tube socks and Birkenstock sandals, and a T-shirt that said DANGER: EDUCATED BLACK MAN.

"Ain't we been bleeding in the streets long enough?" said Jones to no one in particular. "Ain't it time someone give us a Band-Aid? And a bottle of hydrogen peroxide? Brothers, I'm talking about the kind in the brown plastic bottle that cost two dollars and thirty-five cents at CVS. Is that too much to ask?"

A circle of men gathered around him, boasting and arguing. Bets were made, and crumpled bills changed hands as the next round of pickup games got underway. Jones's voice rang out, loud and clear above it all, riffing about politics, music . . . and whatever else crossed his sharp, frenetic, and, some said, crazy mind.

"Yeah," agreed a couple of the gamblers. "You're right."

Dylan tugged on his friends' arms. "Come on, guys. I'm hungry."

"Okay, bro," said Michael, leading them away.

But Elijah stood still, listening. He didn't know if Jones was serious or, like most days, just putting on a show. Because today it seemed like his words were hitting dangerously close to the truth—just ask Ray Shiver's mother. She'd watched her boy bleed, had seen his blood spilled onto the street.

"I don't want to disappoint you, brothers," continued Jones. "But ain't nobody gonna help us. Wanna know how come? Because the best predictor of the future is the past. That's right. And the past says we're on our own."

"Yeah? Why's that?" someone in the crowd said.

Jones stepped onto his white plastic Igloo cooler, the one he kept filled with cold sodas and bottles of Gatorade that he sold for a buck fifty each. "Because nobody ever helped us before, and they ain't gonna do it now." His voice went up another level. "You all understand what I'm saying? You feel me?"

"No, I don't," someone said.

"I ain't bleeding," said another. "Do you see any blood?"

"William." Jones pointed at the nonbeliever, and all eyes turned. "How many bank accounts you got?"

"I don't trust no bank," said William.

"Health insurance?"

"Naw."

"You own a house or rent?"

"What do you think?" said William.

"You see what I'm saying? You're bleeding money and power all over these streets. Every day." Jones lowered his voice. Now he was all kindness and compassion. "It ain't your fault, brother, but it is up to you to fix it."

A murmur went through the small crowd. "How *we* supposed to fix it?"

"I'll show you." Jones reached into his pocket and pulled out a thick roll of bills. He held them up, fanning the edges, like a deck of cards.

The men leaned in close, hypnotized by the fat display.

"This is how we fix it!" Jones stamped his foot like a TV evangelist calling up the power of the Holy Ghost. "This money's healing *my* wounds, brothers. You feel me now? The green gonna heal us and make us strong. The green gonna set us free. Now, who wants to place a bet and make some good healing green of their own?"

The men grumbled. Bills exchanged hands again.

"Got to pay to stay, brothers," said Jones.

"Come on." Elijah appreciated the performance, but he was disappointed that, in the end, it was just a different kind of hustle.

"Dude's good," said Michael.

They crossed the street to Antonio's, the closest if not the cleanest or the best pizza joint in their neighborhood. Inside, they dug deep into their pockets and made a pile of ones and quarters on the counter.

"None of that Hawaiian pizza," said Dylan. "This time I want straight up cheese and pepperoni."

Michael shook his head. "That's why you got no woman."

"You got no woman either, but tell me why I don't got one. Because I'm taking a stand against your nasty Hawaiian pizza?"

"Yeah, but also because you got no imagination. You think too small."

"I'm not thinking small," said Dylan. "I just want what I want. What's wrong with that?"

"Nothing, but a woman likes a man who ain't afraid to stretch his horizons."

"You don't know what you're talking about," said Dylan. "Pizza ain't horizons; it's pizza. Right, Elijah? Tell this fool."

Elijah shrugged and looked at his amazing new shoes. Part of him couldn't believe his good fortune; the other part knew there had to be some kind of a catch. After all, *If something looks too good to be true, it probably is.* That was one of his mother's favorite sayings, and it pained him to admit that most of the time she was right.

After negotiating pizza toppings (half Hawaiian, half pepperoni), the boys crammed into a booth and fell into the time-honored practice of bragging, exaggerating, and telling stories about their victory on the court.

"You remember that big rebound?" said Dylan. "Michael was like King Kong swatting toy airplanes."

Michael raised one of his big paws and waved it in the air movie-monster style. Then he pointed at Elijah and said, "Best play of the game by far was that dunk. That was incredible."

Elijah tried not to smile. "It was the setup. Dylan's bounce pass and your alley-oop. You two can feed me passes like that all day long."

Before walking home, the trio sat on a bench and carefully removed their new shoes. They picked pebbles from the treads and spit-polished scuffmarks. Dylan kissed both of his and finally, with a sigh of regret, returned them to the orange box.

"You really think we can win Hoops?" asked Dylan. "It's a whole different thing, playing in the adult division."

"Yeah," said Elijah. "Didn't you hear what Coach said at the end of the school season? He said we're ready, and if we play like we did at the end of the school season, no one out there is going to stop us."

"Passing game, right?" said Dylan.

"Ball moves faster than the player," said Elijah.

6

MICHAEL WAS UNUSUALLY quiet, and it wasn't until later, after Dylan peeled away from them at his apartment building, that he spoke.

"That dunk you pulled off tonight. I didn't even know you could do that. It was like you changed in front of us. Went up to a whole 'nother level. How's that happen? No, just tell me what it feels like, because I don't think I'll ever know."

Elijah wasn't sure if his friend was proud of him or upset. But he understood what Michael meant, or at least, he thought he did. Because, over the past couple of months, something strange and inexplicable had been happening to Elijah whenever he stepped onto a basketball court. As soon as he picked up a ball, energy began to course and surge through his body, all electric and powerful, muscle fibers burning and twitching with the promise of . . . of what? A scholarship at a good college, like Coach Walters had talked about? Sure, that was great, but it wasn't nearly as strong as his dream.

"I didn't know I could do that, either," said Elijah. "It just happened."

"You got something special, man. Your skills are gonna carry you right on out of here."

"You, too," said Elijah.

"Naw. I got enough skills to hold my own in any neighborhood game, but not like what you got. You got the real thing, Elijah. You're going places."

"Come on, man." Elijah waved his hand dismissively. "Stop blowing smoke."

"I'm serious. It should be a thing of pride; it is for Dylan and me. We talked about it last night, and we're both proud of you and what you're gonna do when you leave here. Coach Walters is, too."

Elijah looked down at his feet. He didn't know how to respond.

After a beat, Michael added, "You can be humble and downplay it all you want, but this is real. It's one of the reasons I pushed to get us them shoes, because you deserve to play your best in some real kicks. You'll see; you're gonna go somewhere."

"Yeah, like where?"

"Anyplace you want. Check it out. The other day I was downtown with my uncle Cole, and I seen this guy who couldn't have been more than a few years older than us. Twenty-three at most. And, like, he got out of this sick-looking BMW, one of them 750s, wearing a two-thousand-dollar suit, Rolex, the works."

"So what? He was rich."

"I asked my uncle what the dude's story was, and he said the guy was just a brother with a MBA or a law degree. Man, I didn't even know what a MBA was! I had to ask him."

"Master of business administration."

"Smart-ass." Michael delivered the slightest shove that sent Elijah reeling off the sidewalk. "Point is, there's, like, other worlds out there. And the doors to them worlds is locked, unless you're like my uncle Cole or that dude with the BMW. And those two busted their butts to get the keys. You know what I mean?"

"You're sounding a little bit like Jones. I'll get you a red Kangol hat."

"Man, don't change the subject. Do you or do you not know what I'm talking about?"

"I do, but if I'm going off to play college ball, they'd better offer me a three-for-one deal. You guys are coming with me."

"Come on, man. Dylan's gonna have to work his hardest just to get a diploma or maybe a GED, 'cause you know the white brother can't read! I love him, but I ain't lying, am I?"

"He can read the pictures in his comics," said Elijah. "And what about you?"

"I'm gonna live with one beautiful woman after the next. They gonna support me because they know that a sexy fat boy got all the love they need."

Elijah laughed and threw an arm over his friend's big shoulders. He'd known that, someday, they would all go their separate ways. But he never could have said it out loud, the way Michael had. And he hadn't thought it would happen so soon. After all, they'd been together since kindergarten. They'd talked about growing old together, settling down in the neighborhood and coaching each other's kids in peewee sports. What kind of a guy would he be if he left all that behind?

"I'm not going to lie," said Elijah. "I want to play college ball. I mean, that stuff you said about doors and keys, I've thought about that a lot. But I don't think I can leave my mom."

"Your moms will kick your butt if you stay because of her. Why do you think she works two jobs? So you can carve out your own little square of pavement and fight the rest of your short, stupid life to protect it?"

"You've been watching too many movies. That's not how it is." Or was it?

"Maybe," said Michael. "But things is changing. Trust me, I know."

"How do you know?"

Michael looked over his shoulder twice in quick succession, a gesture of nervousness that was out of sync with his smooth-talking persona. "You know that shooting on Grider Street?"

"Yeah." Elijah still hadn't told anyone that he'd been at the crime scene. He guessed a part of him couldn't believe it had happened.

"I heard the kid got iced by some gangbanger that calls himself Assassin."

"Okay," said Elijah. "So, what does that prove? Every year there's a different suburban school that gets shot up with a machine gun. Doesn't mean everyone in the suburbs is packing an Uzi."

"No," said Michael. "But maybe this neighborhood is changing if kids like Ray Shiver are getting shot. I'm just saying that pretty soon we're gonna have to choose what side we're on. And your side better be college. So listen. When you go, I want a T-shirt and sweatshirt with the school's name on it. Georgetown, UNLV, UCONN, whatever. Get me the heavyweight ones, right? Double XL, or as I tell the ladies, man-sized."

Elijah gave his friend a bump before turning up the walkway to his house. "If college is my side, what's yours?"

"It ain't gonna be school, I can tell you that much," confided Michael. "And there's no way I'm wearing no corny Burger King uniform, working at a minimum-wage joint. So what's that leave?"

"Lots. The priesthood. Marine Corps. You could be a park ranger, or a shepherd."

"You ain't even close to funny," said Michael.

"Then how come you're laughing?" asked Elijah.

"I ain't; it's just heartburn. And because I'm fat. But seriously, I'll figure something out. I'm a survivor, man. I'll get my own set of keys to them doors we been talking about. I'll show up one day in a big BMW and take you and Dylan out for a steak dinner. Or sushi. You like sushi? My uncle Cole says that's what rich white folks eat."

"Okay," said Elijah. "I'm going home now to wait for my free sushi dinner."

"Later, college boy."

"Later, Michael."

7

ELIJAH AWAKENED CRAVING coffee and eggs, which meant he'd have to make it himself or settle for cold cereal; it was one of the long-standing rules of the house. His mother cooked dinner, but for breakfast, he was on his own.

He pulled on sweats and got to work in the kitchen, scrambling a few eggs while frying a pan of onions and red peppers. He stirred in the eggs and then scooped coffee grounds into the machine's paper filter, waiting for the omelet to set.

"Smells good." His mother set the table with cream, sugar, and Tabasco for the eggs, moving with the briskness and efficiency of a waitress, one of the two jobs she held in service of being a single mom. She sat down at the kitchen island, her face strained with worry. "Did you hear about that poor boy who was killed on Grider Street?"

"Yes."

"Did you know him?"

"We went to school together. I knew him well enough to say hi."

She shook her head, her posture tense. "How come you didn't say anything?"

"I didn't know what to say, Mom. I read in the paper that

they're doing a big investigation. But that doesn't change anything. Ray was a good kid. He followed all the rules. It doesn't make sense."

"It makes me very sad," said his mother. "What if something like that happened to you or one of your friends?"

He nodded, understanding the source of her concern.

"I feel like I'm supposed to have some answers for you, Elijah, but I don't. Does Coach Walters talk to you boys about gangs? About staying safe?"

"He does, but Michael, Dylan, and I look out for each other." They exchanged smiles. His mother was still a pretty woman, especially when she was happy. But he noticed lines of worry and stress on her forehead and at the corners of her eyes. He wished her life could be easier, but how do you stop a single mother in West Baltimore from working hard and worrying about her only son? Maybe that is her job, but he wanted to do whatever he could to make it better.

She took a careful sip of her coffee. "Elijah, there's somebody from church I'd like you to meet."

"Who?" For a moment he entertained the terrible fear that his mother was about to set him up with a girl, someone's sweet, cross-eyed goddaughter who sang in the church choir and collected ceramic cat figurines. In short, a nice person but not anyone he'd want to date.

"He's a friend of Pastor Fredericks. He just retired from the military and bought an old house that needs a lot of work."

"Are you talking about a job?"

"No, I just thought he could use your help. His daughter is coming to stay with him for the summer, and the yard is a mess. He wants it to look nice for the girl, which I think is sweet. He lives on Prospect."

"I know where Prospect is. That's a rough neighborhood. So why wouldn't I get paid? I did last time."

The summer past he had painted an entire garage while the owner, a retired dentist with a fluffy, white Afro, had supervised every brushstroke from his nylon lawn chair. *You missed a spot,* the guy had said about 137 times. Or, *You're going too heavy there; it's going to drip. See! There's a drip.*

"No, I'm not asking you to do this for money," she said. "I'm asking you to do it because, frankly, I'm worried about the world we live in. And I think it would be a nice thing to help a new neighbor. It's just a little yard work. And maybe someday, if we ever move, someone will help us."

"Why would we move?" said Elijah. But he knew. If Ray Shiver could get shot in the street, then so could he, or his friends. And for his mother, that was more than enough of a reason.

"We're not moving. I'm just saying that it's nice to pay it forward sometimes. And this man is desperate for some help; he's asked me half a dozen times when you can get started. I told him you'd come by this afternoon."

"I'm practicing basketball at eleven," said Elijah.

"Then you can meet him at two o'clock," said his mother.

Elijah thought it over while sipping his coffee. Inwardly he groaned at the thought of meeting an old military guy from his mother's church. And just how much help would he need? A little yard work would be fine, but anything more would cut into his training time. Not good, because if he was going take his team all the way—which he had to do if his father was going to hear about it and come watch him play—he'd have to stay focused. But as a rule he did not argue with his mother; she worked too hard for that. "Okay, Mom. I'll help him."

"His name is Mr. Banks," said his mother. "I think you two will get along just fine, and spending a few less hours hanging around with your friends isn't going to hurt you. I'll bet Dylan's brother, Marvin, wouldn't have gotten arrested if he'd been working for Mr. Banks instead of running the streets."

"I'm not Marvin, Mom. And neither is Dylan." Elijah sprinkled shredded cheese and folded the omelet into a perfect half-moon. He garnished it with a sliced cherry tomato and then slid it onto his mother's plate.

"Heavens, the boy can cook!" she said. "This looks delicious. Thank you."

And with that, the matter was closed. Elijah wanted to explain that playing basketball or, more accurately, practicing with his friends for the tournament, was not a gateway to dealing drugs or getting arrested.

"So, what did this guy do in the military?"

"You know, I'm not entirely sure. You should ask him; I bet he'd be happy to tell you about it, if you're curious."

"I'm not," said Elijah. "I was just wondering." He started making his own eggs, hoping Mr. Banks, the retired military guy, didn't interfere too much with his training schedule.

6

NEARING PROSPECT STREET, Elijah wondered about this Mr. Banks. How old was he, and why couldn't he do his own yard work? Elijah soon stood outside the small bungalow on Prospect Street that was being reclaimed by weeds and shrubs. The house was on a large double lot that was almost completely overgrown. A pair of ceramic garden gnomes peeked out from under a ragged boxwood, their tiny necks encircled with creeper vine. He looked at the neighboring houses for comparison. Both of them were freshly painted, picture-perfect. "Jesus," he muttered out loud. "This place is hopeless."

Heavy footsteps fell behind him, and he turned.

"Who are you?" said a lean, middle-aged man who stood ramrod straight, eyes blazing with intensity and suspicion. His dark brown skin was deeply creased and was shiny with sweat. He'd wrapped a white towel around his neck, the ends tucked into his plain gray T-shirt.

"Um, I'm supposed to . . . ," muttered Elijah.

"Better speak up, son." The man removed his towel; cords of muscle and tendon stood out. "You're on my property, and I don't know you."

"My mother goes to Pastor Fredericks's church," said Elijah quickly. "She said you needed help with your yard."

A flash of recognition. The man's face smoothed, but he still looked far from friendly. "I remember now. What's your name?"

"Elijah. Elijah Thomas."

"Right."

Elijah had the distinct feeling that the man was seeing straight into him, or through him. He didn't like it and was about to say something, but the man turned abruptly and headed up the uneven, cracked walkway that led to the front steps.

"Better come on in," said the man. "We'll talk."

Elijah followed him up a set of equally wrecked concrete steps and into a tiled coatroom that was surprisingly clean and ordered. A canvas jacket hung on a hook, below which stood a pair of black leather engineer boots; they looked well worn but were buffed to a low gloss. The man unlaced his running shoes and lined them up next to the boots, both pairs pointing at the door, ready for action. Elijah took his own shoes off and then followed Mr. Banks into the living room, the surfaces of which gleamed in the morning light.

"In here," said the man.

They walked across oak floors that were undisturbed by furniture. And past scrubbed white walls devoid of artwork or pictures. Aside from a few cardboard boxes stacked in a corner, and an ironing board, the place appeared empty.

"I'm Banks." The man stopped, turned, and extended his hand.

Elijah expected the kind of bone-crushing shake that guys often used to show how tough they were or, more to the point, how tough they *thought* they were. But Banks's was in the category of solidly firm.

"I'm Elijah."

Again, the man looked at him a little too closely, sizing him up. "Are you an athlete?"

"I play basketball."

"Do you lift weights?" said Banks.

"No, I just play ball. Sometimes I run home from the courts."

"Hmm. You any good?"

"I think so." Banks turned and headed around a corner to the kitchen. The fridge was empty except for beer bottles, a carton of orange juice, and a single lime. The appliance's inside light cast the edges of Banks's shirt in a yellow glow; he stared at the shelves, apparently unable to decide between the three choices. At last, he took the carton and poured himself a glass of juice.

As an afterthought, he said, "You want some?"

"No, thanks." Despite his thirst, Elijah didn't feel welcome enough in this man's house to accept anything from him. Mr. Banks wasn't desperate for his help. *Suspicious* was a better word. He decided that whatever this guy's story was, it couldn't be good. Scanning the kitchen counter, Elijah counted a dozen empty bottles—dead soldiers, he'd heard them called—and a couple of Chinese take-out cartons. There was a small framed picture, too, with a very pretty young woman in it. If it was Banks's daughter, there was no resemblance.

"You're going to be big," said Banks, still doing his looking-right-through-you trick. "How big is your father?"

"I don't know. I don't remember him."

"I shouldn't have asked," said Banks.

Elijah noted that it wasn't exactly an apology. "I shouldn't have asked" was different from saying "I'm sorry I asked."

"It's fine," Elijah said, even though it wasn't fine, because now he had to contend with certain thoughts and questions that were very hard to get rid of. They had a tendency to swirl in his head and, eventually, darken his mood. He looked down at his feet, and then, hating himself for being affected by something that was so far out of his control, he glared hard at Banks. "How big is *your* father?"

35

"He was a wiry bastard, like me, but he really knew how to throw a punch." Absently he rubbed his chin, which was covered in gray stubble.

"Oh."

In the awkward silence that ensued, Banks drained his glass and motioned for Elijah to follow. "I'll show you what I need done. I won't lie: it's a lot." They walked out of the kitchen and through the back door. "Are you afraid of hard work, like most people these days?"

"No."

"Hmph." He seemed not to believe him. "Tools are back here. The shed's ready to fall down, so be careful; I don't want any emergency-room trips or insurance claims."

7

THEY FOUGHT THEIR way through the backyard, which was a jungle of thornbushes and weeds. The lawn, or what should have been a lawn, was bare dirt, packed hard except where some roots and stones poked through. At the very back of the property, against a rotting picket fence, stood a crooked wooden structure built on a cinder block foundation. Its doors hung askew on bent hinges, spilling the shed's collection of rusty shovels and hand tools onto the ground.

Elijah hesitated, wondering just how badly his mother had set him up. Was she really expecting him to do this much work for free? That would be crazy.

"Having second thoughts?" said Banks.

"I didn't say that." But he was certainly thinking it. He picked up a pair of clippers and tested them out. At first the arms wouldn't budge, but when he jammed them against his chest, the hinge broke free with a small puff of rust.

"I understand," said Banks. "I'll think of something to tell your mother so it will come back on me."

"Mr. Banks," said Elijah. "If you don't want me here, just say so."

"To be honest," said Banks, "I don't. I'd rather hire a

professional landscaping crew. But I couldn't say no to your mother; she was very persistent."

"What do you mean?" said Elijah, setting down the clippers.

"She asked me half a dozen times," said Banks.

"Okay." Elijah started to leave. "I'll tell her something came up. It's no problem."

Banks scratched his chin again. "Hold on. Hold on." He waved his hands at the tangled jungle of his new yard. "You're already here. Why don't you have at it, and we'll talk later about what I should pay you."

"You don't need to pay me," said Elijah. "My mom wouldn't approve of that."

"Why not?" said Banks.

"Against her principles, I guess." Elijah smiled, unable to hide his amusement. Apparently his mother's good-neighbor practices were too revolutionary for Banks's ordered, military mind.

"That's nice and all," said Banks, "but I don't like to owe anybody anything. If you're going to work for me, I'm paying."

Elijah shrugged. He picked up the clippers again and began cutting. At first, he lopped off stalks and branches at random, hitting anything close. But soon he observed a pattern and worked more deliberately.

Banks pulled out a cigar and a lighter from one of his pockets and fired up. He stood out of Elijah's way, looking distracted and pensive at the same time, blowing rings into the humid air and watching them float upward until they grew large and disappeared. After a few minutes, he stubbed out his cigar into the hard-packed ground and went inside.

Elijah cut all manner of growth until his shirt was soaked with sweat and his eyes stung. When he had enough branches, he cut and broke them into arm-length pieces and piled them by the fence. Banks came out to check on him once, carrying a glass of ice water. Sweat beaded and dripped off the sides. "I'm surprised you're still here."

"Why wouldn't I be?" said Elijah.

"I thought you'd have quit by now," he said. "It's a lot of work."

Elijah took the glass and gulped down the water. "I'm not a quitter."

"Maybe not, but willingness to work is a vanishing trait. Most people these days are kind of . . ."

"Kind of what?" said Elijah.

"Lazy, and weak." The older man took a seat on one of a pair of overturned buckets. He gestured for Elijah to sit on the other. "But I probably shouldn't talk that way anymore. What I meant to say is 'good job.' So far."

"Thanks," said Elijah. "I think."

They sat silently. Elijah remembered the painting job with the white-haired dentist; compared to Banks, that guy seemed like a gem. Still, if Elijah was going to try to tough it out, then perhaps he should make an effort to get to know Banks. "What did you do in the military? Were you a soldier?"

"No. I was an accountant, in the army. Papers and files. Boring stuff. I sat at a desk and went to meetings, same as everyone else in the civilian world."

"You don't look like an accountant," said Elijah, observing again the ropes of muscles on the man's neck and arms.

"Ha. What's an accountant look like?"

"Bad suit, briefcase, comb-over. A little soft in the middle." Elijah couldn't imagine someone like Banks buttoned up in a suit, sitting behind a desk. Then again, he couldn't really imagine a guy like him doing anything else, either. Especially if it involved working with people, or speaking in complete sentences. Elijah drank deeply; the water was a cold shock to the back of his throat.

"I've got some bad suits," said Banks.

"Did you get to travel?"

"Sure, but army bases all look the same. Same food. Same people. Same rules. Same green uniforms."

"Sounds fascinating." Elijah stood and picked up the clippers; he'd decided that more backbreaking work in ninety-five-degree heat would be easier than trying to make conversation.

Banks pulled a piece of paper from his back pocket. "Right. Here's the list of all the things I want you to do with the house and the yard, along with how much time each one should take."

Elijah took the paper and saw a bunch of tasks written in careful black print that looked like it had come from a typewriter. The letters were so small and uniform that he could hardly believe a person had penned them. Across from each odd job, Banks had listed the number of hours he expected the task to take.

Clearing out shrubs	10 hours
Spread topsoil & seed back lawn	8 hours
Mow and edge front and side lawns	1 hour
Clean gutters	2 hours
Power wash house	6 hours
Power wash garage	3 hours
Break up concrete drive	5 hours
Stack concrete chunks	2 hours
Lay new pavers	10 hours

"I'll pay you a dollar an hour over minimum, cash, at the end of each day. If you finish everything on the list and do a good job, you get an automatic raise of another dollar an hour. How's that sound?"

"Sounds fine," said Elijah. "But I still can't take your money."

Banks looked at him and scowled. "That's not negotiable. I'm paying. You decide what to do with it and what to tell your mother. Donate it to charity. Set it on fire. That's your business. How early do you get up?"

"I'm done with school now, so I can get here by nine."

"Make it seven-thirty," said Banks. "You can have half an hour for lunch. Quitting time will be four-thirty, and make sure your work area is cleaned up and the tools put away in the shed before you leave. Those are my rules."

Elijah stared. "Seven-thirty? That's pretty early."

"It's not even close to early. Five o'clock is early. And if you're late, even once . . ."

"I won't be late," said Elijah.

"We'll see," said Banks. "You had enough for one day?"

"I can work a little more."

Elijah stopped at seven o'clock and put the tools back into the shed. He stood for a moment, regarding the product of his efforts: a pile of sticks, limbs, and root clusters that towered above his six feet and four inches. The yard looked completely different, like it had been tamed. He slung his pack over his shoulders and made his way around the side of the house, then hit the pavement in a loose jog, taking note of the little red Fiat ragtop that had just parked out front.

"Look at you!" Banks called to someone—not him—from the crumbling front steps. His voice was unusually loud and cheerful.

Elijah jogged backward, watching the tall, pretty girl stepping out from behind the car door, and Banks walking toward her.

"Hi, Daddy," she said, throwing her arms around Banks's leathery neck.

Banks looked like a statue, but after a moment the hug softened him. He wrapped his arms around his daughter, and then lifted her off the ground. "Hi, baby. I'm so glad to see you. Come on, let me show you the house."

10

ELIJAH STOPPED AT Antonio's for two slices and then crossed the street to the Battlegrounds. He checked the string of texts from Michael: "Where are you, man?" "Dylan's at my house watching some TV." And "My moms made lasagna. Come on over."

Elijah ate his pizza while waiting his turn on the bench. He joined a pickup game with a bunch of beefed-up older guys who threw as many elbows as they did shots. The most vicious of the bunch was well known at the Battlegrounds as Bull, on account of his thick neck and the gold nose ring.

At the start of the game, Bull purposefully matched up against Elijah and got in close enough to whisper, so that no one else could hear. "You ain't nothing, you feel me? This is *my* court."

Bull's story was that he'd been recruited to play for the University of Maryland but had been promptly thrown out for assaulting the coach—and the team's star forward. Ever since, he'd been hanging out at the Battlegrounds dishing out threats to every talented young player with the audacity to stand against him. Elijah offered a slight smile. Like it or not, goons were plentiful, and trash talk was a part of the game. Among his own crew, Michael was the reigning champ. Elijah seldom participated; the way he figured, talk was energy, and he wanted all of his energy to go into the game.

At the top of the key, Elijah dribbled loosely. He could feel the other players—on both teams—watching, waiting for someone to twitch and make his move. It was like a fight scene in the old Bruce Lee movies he and Dylan used to watch, where Bruce and the most cold-blooded bad guy would square off in mortal combat. Elijah had always admired how cool and relaxed the martial artist was, like his fear had been surgically removed, leaving only the calm resolve of a righteous badass dealing out lessons. Elijah hoped that someday he could play ball with that kind of attitude. So, like Master Lee, Elijah flexed his neck from side to side until a vertebra popped, all the while working the ball slowly, effortlessly, like a rhythmic invitation for Bull to charge.

The big man held his ground, but the tension in the air was palpable and growing with each second. Elijah let the ball drop from his outstretched hand slowly, inexorably, like a piece of fruit, detached and falling from its branch. Bull lunged, but Elijah was slippery with movement and skipped the ball neatly around his back. He anticipated the impact from Bull's shoulder and, at the last possible moment, rolled away from it without any loss of momentum. He banged the ball, two quick punctuations off the pavement, and then glided underneath the steel for an easy layup.

"That's what I'm talking about!" said one of Elijah's teammates, slapping skin.

Bull's teammates tried to console him, only to have their hands shoved away. "Man, get off me." His flaring, ringed nostrils seemed to promise the delivery of a fistful of pain on the next possession.

"Make it, you take it, baby." One of Elijah's teammates handled the check-in and then fed him a short pass. Elijah feigned a jumper but never got to finish it because a crushing elbow dropped him hard onto the blacktop. Elijah rolled onto his side, tasting blood.

"My court," said Bull. "You've got game but no heart."

Elijah felt around with his tongue for any loose teeth; the inside of his mouth seemed to be in order but was pulsing from the impact. He felt consumed with anger and the incomprehensible need to hit somebody. Sure Bull was bigger and stronger, but so what? He couldn't foul him like that and get away with it. But then he heard a quieter, calmer voice from deep inside. *What are you going to do when someone fouls you in the tournament? Fight and get disqualified? And never make it to the finals? No, you've got to be the bigger man and play your game. Use your anger to get stronger. Better.*

Elijah rose slowly. And rather than getting up swinging, or standing chest to chest trading insults with the ringed, muscle-bound fool, he looked Bull in the eyes and slapped him lightly on the shoulder, as he would one of his friends. "Nice defense."

"Ha!" howled one of the guy's teammates. "You hear that?"

The game restarted with a new level of intensity. It was no longer about the winner or the score—if it had ever been. It all came down to a single question: Who was going to emerge as the top dog of that particular square of asphalt? Who was going to own it?

Elijah answered by nailing a clean three-pointer. Moments later, he followed with a fast drive up the middle. He dribbled toward Bull's weaker left side, but before he could break through, a thick muscled forearm came out of nowhere and caught him under his chin. Elijah's body whiplashed backward. He went down hard, hands clamped reflexively in the universal gesture of someone who is choking.

"How do you like that defense?" asked Bull.

Elijah dragged himself to his knees. He sucked the pain down deep, to a place where there was no room for calmness or reason. Instead, there was only reaction, the primitive urge to lash out and fight. He delivered a perfect straight punch, the muscles along his wrist, forearm, and triceps locking together at the precise moment his fist connected with Bull's balls.

"Oaf!" The big man lost his air in a quick rush and doubled over at the waist.

The blood was rising within Elijah, pumping up his arms and shoulders so that they could finish the job. He knew it had to be finished, because someone like Bull would have no respect for mercy.

"Get him," offered one of Elijah's teammates.

"Yeah," said another. "We're sick of his crap."

Think, said the calm voice. *You need to think your way out of this.*

Elijah knew what the situation demanded of him, what most guys on the court would do. He was supposed to beat fear into his enemy. But he didn't care about Bull, nor was he interested in having people fear him; all he wanted was to be respected for his skill and ability on the court. Slowly Elijah uncurled his fingers and gave Bull a gentle shove; the big man fell over and lay still, knees tucked protectively into his chest like a little boy hurt on the playground.

Elijah turned his back and began walking away. He made it as far as the bench on the sidelines before Bull's pained, choked words reached him: "This ain't over."

11

ELIJAH RUBBED HIS throat and wished Michael and Dylan were with him. He scanned the Battlegrounds parking lot to see if Bull or his friends had a car; that way, he could keep an eye out, in case the big man decided to seek revenge. But the lot was empty, save for the black Mercedes he'd seen before. Elijah noticed the same hooded figure leaning against the front bumper, beckoning.

Elijah pointed to his chest. "Me?"

The figure nodded.

"From bad to worse," muttered Elijah. Slowly he made his way over to the shining black sedan parked at the far corner of the lot, out of reach of the bright fluorescent lights.

When he was about fifteen feet away, the guy lightly tapped the car's hood with the barrel of a small, silver handgun. "Sit down."

Elijah went close enough to touch the front bumper, but he did not sit. Under other circumstances, he might have corrected the guy. *Don't tell me what to do,* he might have said. But everything about this situation—the gun, the remote location, the creepy vibe—it all told him that he should move slowly and, above all else, keep his mouth shut.

"I want to talk business with you," said the guy.

"Okay." *What business? This isn't good. Find a way to get out of here.*

A finger emerged from the hoodie's cuff, pointing at the courts. "You got some serious skills with that ball. Where'd you learn?"

"Right here," said Elijah. "I've been playing here since I was six."

"Little brothers don't play at the Battlegrounds."

"The guys used to chase me away. Eventually they gave up and let me into some games."

The guy's laugh was high and reedy, forced through his teeth. "I seen how you handled Bull. It ain't easy to drop a man like that. Brother's all roided up." He patted the hood again. "Sit down, man. We're just talking."

Elijah sat reluctantly on the hood. "He clotheslined me; I had to do something."

"Uh-huh. Respect. But you know he's going to come after you."

"I know."

"So what are you going to do about it?"

"Hit him in the nuts again, I guess."

Another forced laugh. "That's funny. It would have been easier to finish him when you had the chance, though. You should always deal with a problem the right way, and then it don't come back. You feel me?"

Elijah nodded, even though he thought it was a stupid philosophy, unless you wanted to end up dead or in prison. At least that was how it had worked for Dylan's brother.

The gun disappeared into the hoodie's pocket, only to be replaced with a glossy picture. "This is for you. A message from my boss who's interested in you."

Elijah held it by the corners as though the photograph might burn his fingers. The cropped image showed the front of his house, on Eutaw Place. And as clear as day, on the front steps, was his mother. She must have been returning from work, because she was still wearing her uniform for her first job, at the bank—a dark skirt and white blouse, with her hair pinned up in the back.

"Why do you have a picture . . ."

But the gun was out again, poking him in his upper arm. "Easy, brother. I'm just a middleman, delivering a message. And this ain't no threat."

Elijah didn't believe him for a minute. "Then what is it?"

"Just something to get your attention. Go on and flip it over." On the back, someone had written the house number, along with his mother's two work addresses. "That's to let you know your moms is easy to find, if someone wants to find her."

Elijah studied the addresses, trying hard not to let his fingers shake, trying not to show the fear that was steadily taking over his body.

"So, do I got your attention?" asked the guy.

"Yes." Elijah stood up and forced the word through clenched teeth. He wondered how hard of a punch he could throw, and if he could deliver it before the gun went off. It wasn't a serious thought, because he knew that he would sit still and listen to whatever else the guy had to say. But his right biceps twitched, as though the readiness of the fibers could override his brain and hijack the situation.

"Good." The gun barrel made a small circle in the air. "That's the message."

"That's it? Who's your boss? Why is he interested in me?"

"We'll talk again, when it's time. Understand?"

"Yes," said Elijah.

"Now get lost."

Elijah willed his frozen legs to move. He walked slowly from the car in measured strides. Twenty feet. Thirty feet. And then, no longer able to hold himself back, he broke into a full-out sprint. He ran as fast as he could, the image of his pretty mother standing on the steps outside their house burned into his mind. "Please," he said out loud. "Let her be okay."

12

UP THE WALKWAY, gasping for breath; then Elijah was working his key in the lock.

This ain't no threat.

It had felt like one.

Inside, he leaned against the back of the door before sliding the bolt and chain. His heart beat wildly until he found his mother asleep in front of the TV. The house was quiet and orderly. He watched her sleep for several minutes, trying to convince himself that there was no real danger, that his heart could return to its normal rhythm. Elijah covered his mother with a blanket and turned off the TV.

Upon reaching his bedroom, he poked distractedly at the orange Nike box on his dresser trying to make sense of all that had happened. First a fight with Bull, then a threat from the guy in the hoodie. And then there were the shoes. He didn't believe there was a connection, but what kind of anonymous guy would front twelve hundred dollars for sneakers to a bunch of high school kids? It made no sense, unless there was a catch, something they had to do to pay the guy back. Like what?

Just something to get your attention.

Well, the guy had Elijah's attention.

He took out his phone and pulled up Michael's contact.

"Hey." Michael picked up on the fourth ring. "What's up?"

"Michael, tell me about your friend who bought us the shoes."

"What, this again?" said Michael, slightly annoyed. "I told you, he's a businessman. Ain't nothing illegal about having a sponsor, if that's what you're bugging about. Lots of teams have sponsors."

"Then you should be able to tell me his name."

"His name's Money."

"Money?"

"That's his street name. I don't know his real one."

"This may sound weird, but what kind of car does he drive? Does he have a black Mercedes?"

Michael paused for a moment, thinking. "Naw, that ain't him. Money drives a white Escalade." His tone dropped to show how hurt his feelings were. "You don't trust me, do you?"

"It's not that. I just met this dude in a black Mercedes and wondered if it was your guy. But he definitely didn't have an Escalade."

"But you're still bugging about the shoes. Listen, man, I told you it's cool. Why can't you trust me on this?"

"I do." Elijah took in a long, deep breath. "But do we really need a sponsor? We made it to the semifinals last year with old shoes and white T-shirts. Maybe that's who we are. Maybe that's good enough and we don't need Kobe 10s."

"I feel you," said Michael. "Humble roots, right? But we're getting older, you know what I mean? At some point a man has to represent and show he's more than another broke-ass neighborhood kid. Besides, I can't give them shoes back; it'll look bad. I don't want to offend the brother."

"I'll do it, then. I'll give them back. It'll be on me."

"No, it still comes back to me, and I don't want to get on

Money's bad side; he said he might be able to hook us up with jobs after the tournament."

Elijah didn't want a job from someone named Money, but he let it go. Why couldn't he tell his best friend about what had just happened to him? He wanted to, but somehow, he knew that Michael couldn't help him. He was on his own with the hooded guy in the Mercedes.

"Listen, man," said Michael. "Just relax and enjoy the shoes. It's all good, I swear."

"Okay."

"So how come you didn't come by? Where were you?"

"I had to help out my mom's friend with some house stuff. Afterwards I went to the Battlegrounds, then home."

"House stuff? There's, like, less than two weeks before the tournament. How come you're starting a job?"

"It's a long story. Basically I promised my mom. You know how that is."

"I do. Gotta respect the moms. Who is it, some old lady?"

"A guy. Retired. Bought a house that's all jacked up." Elijah felt drained by the events of the day. His body ached from physical work, and then there was the pounding he'd received at the hands of Bull. His throat still hurt from being clotheslined. He wouldn't be surprised if in the morning he had several elbow-shaped bruises on his arms and ribs.

"Elijah," said Michael. "You still there?"

"Yeah," said Elijah. "But I got to get going." He wished he could rewind the events of the day and play them over differently. If only he had skipped the Battlegrounds, he wouldn't have gotten into a fight with Bull. Nor would he have sat on the hood of the Mercedes, *not* being threatened. But even if he could rewrite the day, the picture of his mom on their front steps would still exist. There was no way to change that.

"Okay, bro," said Michael.

13

THROUGHOUT ELIJAH'S DREAMS, a cold, flat voice replayed the same line.

We'll talk again. When it's time.

In the morning, he pulled the covers over his head to shut out the alarm. It was time to get up if he was going to stick to Banks's ridiculous military schedule. Seven-thirty was a deal breaker, and he thought of all the reasons he should stay home. In addition to the fact that school had just ended and he needed a break, there was the issue of the practice sessions he wanted to have. However, practicing at the Battlegrounds brought to mind the two people he most wanted to avoid—Bull and the guy in the black hoodie.

Elijah dragged himself out of bed and dressed in his oldest T-shirt and pair of jeans. Then he made his way to the kitchen to grab a quick breakfast and make sandwiches.

His mother was busy mixing water and a fine dark powder in a tiny pot. "Do you want to have some Turkish coffee with me?"

"Is that what that is?" He peered into the pot, sniffed. "I think I'm good with regular coffee. Or better yet, some OJ."

She placed the pot over a burner and stirred it. "I wanted to try something different. Who knows, maybe I'll like it. And maybe I'll be adventurous and go to Turkey one day. I'll sit in an outdoor café and order a cup. A real cup served with two cubed sweets."

"Since when do you want to go to Turkey?"

"I'm not sure that I do. But right now I'm happy to dream about going to Turkey. Sometimes the dream is more important than the thing itself. Does that make any sense?"

It did, which was exactly why he didn't speak of his dreams about his father. They were too important. Besides, the events of the prior day were still fresh in his mind. He wished there were a way to tell her about the hooded guy and the picture. But where to start? *Hey, Mom, some nameless thug has a picture of you and knows where we live. I don't know who he is or what he wants, but I just thought you should know.*

No, it would be better to deal with it on his own. As soon as he figured out how. "I'm going to work at Mr. Banks's house." He grabbed his backpack, phone, and keys.

"Oh, good. I knew you two would hit it off. Isn't he nice?"

Elijah smiled. "Well, I wouldn't say he's nice, but he does need lots of help. You were right about that."

"Can you stay for breakfast?" She turned the stove burner off and pulled out a carton of eggs, milk, and a loaf of bread from the fridge. "I'll cook today. You're doing a good thing. Plus, I don't get to see you anymore."

"No, Mom. I've got to go. But will you do me a favor?"

"Sure. What is it?"

"Keep the doors locked, even when you're home, okay?"

"Why?" His mother scowled. "It's that shooting, isn't it?"

"Maybe," he said. "I just think we should be careful."

14

ELIJAH JOGGED SLOWLY past the Battlegrounds, keeping an eye out for danger. But the park was empty. He'd never been there so early, before the sun had charged the concrete and the surrounding buildings with its heat. It was peaceful, and he wished he'd brought a ball so he could have the place all to himself. It would be nice to drain twenty or thirty shots while everyone else was still asleep. It would be a private thing, without noise or competition. A little piece of time without worries or responsibilities.

He resumed jogging and arrived at Banks's house at seven-thirty sharp.

"You're almost late." Banks sat on the porch steps in his gray T-shirt, a stub of a cigar clamped between his teeth.

Elijah checked the time on his cell. "Seven-thirty. I'm right on time."

Banks pointed to a row of tools laid out neatly on a green canvas tarp: a sledgehammer, a five-foot steel pry bar, safety glasses, and leather work gloves. Next to the gloves was a clean white envelope.

"What's this stuff for?" asked Elijah.

"The envelope's your pay for yesterday and today," said Banks. "The tools are for a new driveway."

"I'm going to put in a new driveway with a sledgehammer?"

"No," said Banks. "You're going to remove the old concrete with a sledgehammer. Unless that's too physical for you."

Elijah got the distinct impression Banks wanted him to fail, which strengthened his resolve to prove that he wasn't a quitter. "Just show me what you want me to do."

Banks shrugged, then hefted the sledgehammer into a long, looping swing. The concrete gave under the impact, spitting up several fist-sized chunks and a small cloud of dust. He hauled back for another powerful swing.

"Okay, I got it," said Elijah, grabbing the tool from Banks. In a single motion, he popped the sledge off his shoulder, slid his right hand down the wooden handle, and let it rip. The steel head cracked off the concrete but didn't produce so much as a crack.

"That's a cream puff of a swing." Banks chewed his cigar and scratched his beard stubble. "You've got to find a weak spot, like that crack there."

Elijah swung again, harder; the crack widened. Once more, this time lengthening the arc of travel, stretching it high above his head at its apex. The blow dislodged two large pieces.

"Better," said Banks grudgingly. "Stack the loose chunks in the backyard. Make sure to break 'em up so they're small enough to carry. And put that money away before one of the neighbor kids steals it." He walked away and disappeared into the garage at the top of the driveway.

Elijah spent the next four hours pounding the concrete into irregular, fifty-pound slabs, and then working them loose with a pry bar. He tried to carry bigger pieces, but they proved too difficult. Once, he staggered under the weight of a monster and nearly dropped it on his toe. Smaller pieces were easier but effectively doubled the amount of time it would take him to finish.

So he worked with fifty-pound chunks, counting off an average of eighteen steps to the backyard. It was like doing weighted lunges, only to the tune of a hundred and seventy sets, compared with the gym standard of three. After each trip, he muscled the sledge into the air and then brought it crashing down. It felt good, especially when he imagined hammering away at the hood of the black Mercedes.

"Did that get your attention?" he said out loud. "Stay the hell away from my mother and me." He brought down the sledge again and again, but stopped when an unfamiliar voice called out from behind.

"Excuse me, but who exactly are you talking to?"

Elijah turned to see a young woman around eighteen or nineteen—the one he'd seen getting out of the red Fiat—standing a few feet away. She had long straight hair and wore stylish black glasses and a T-shirt that said "FBI" in big letters. She handed him a glass of iced tea.

"Thanks," said Elijah.

"My dad talks to himself, too. It's no big deal. Doesn't mean that you're crazy." Her smooth, pretty face broke into a smile. "Or it doesn't mean you're *that* crazy."

Elijah drank, then wiped his sweaty face and forehead on his shirtsleeve. "You're Banks's daughter?"

"I prefer Kerri," she said. "I'd shake your hand, but you're too sweaty. Is that normal?"

Elijah looked at the backs of his forearms, which glistened with perspiration. He tried to think of something to say, but Kerri turned away, walking back toward the house.

"Bye."

WHEN ELIJAH STOPPED for lunch, his shoulder and back muscles quivered with exhaustion, but he felt good. He devoured his sandwiches and then worked some more.

Elijah levered the pieces loose, and then carried them into the small backyard. The edges were rough and tore at his T-shirt and bare arms; his skin was covered in scratches, abrasions, and the fine powder of concrete dust.

Banks came out the back door and grunted hello. In his hand he jiggled a glass of yellow liquid and ice cubes.

"Is that lemonade?"

"It's beer and lime juice. Lots of vitamin C for my health."

"Like the cigars," said Elijah, wondering if the man had any sense of humor or if the army had surgically removed it along with his personality.

"Exactly."

Banks lit up a cigar and sipped his beer. "When you finish busting up all the concrete, I'll pick up pavers from Home Depot. You think you can figure out how to put them in?"

"Probably. I do all the work at my mother's house, and I've been taking Building Trades at school."

"Good. You met my daughter earlier?"

Elijah nodded.

"No offense, but keep your distance," said Banks.

"How could I be offended by that?" asked Elijah.

"It's my job to keep her off the radar of any knuckleheads."

"Uh-huh," said Elijah.

"Good." Banks took a final puff of his cigar before stubbing it out under his heel. "I figured you'd understand." He pulled a white envelope from his back pocket—the same one Elijah had forgotten on the green tarp—and handed it over in lieu of saying goodbye. "Seven-thirty tomorrow. Don't be late."

15

AT HOME ELIJAH opened the envelope and counted $111.13. He explained to his mother that Banks insisted on paying him, and they made a quick deal. Two-thirds of his pay would go into his savings account for college; the rest he could spend on himself. And tonight that meant the movies with Michael and Dylan. Big buckets of salty, extra-butter popcorn, and boxes of candy.

As usual, Dylan brought his coveted NCAA replica ball with him, and they passed it back and forth as they walked. The ball worked its way from hand to hand and around their backs like a quarter floating across a magician's knuckles. Occasionally one of the boys would say the word *switch*, and the ball would change directions. And if someone said *bump*, the ball would skip over the boy in the middle. They didn't even think of it as a game anymore; it was just something they did to pass the time, and it came to them as naturally as walking.

In the theater's crowded lobby, Elijah found himself scanning the crowd, studying everyone in a dark hoodie. He knew how unlikely it was for the guy in the Mercedes to show up at the premier of the new X-Men movie, but anything was possible.

"Who are you looking for?" asked Dylan.

"Your mother," said Elijah reflexively. "She was going to sit with me and hold my hand during the scary parts."

Michael howled with laughter at the joke that never grew old—at least not if you were a seventeen-year-old boy hanging out with your two best friends. Elijah laughed, too, and wondered what would become of the three of them after graduation. They had sworn to stick together, but even now, at the end of their junior year, there were signs. Michael was becoming elusive and spent increasing amounts of time by himself, talking on his cell phone. And Dylan had plans for community college, even though he'd barely passed the eleventh grade.

As for Elijah, in May he'd gotten a money order for fifty-two dollars and fifty cents, made out to the College Board, and had registered to take the SAT exam. His mother was the smartest person he knew, but she'd never been to college—which meant she couldn't really help him with the application process. For more than three hours he'd sat cramped at a miniature desk in the gymnasium, filling in bubbles with a number two pencil. But as stupid as Elijah had felt, he'd known he had to do it, and that soon it would pay off.

And, just like the coach of his high school team had predicted, he'd begun receiving letters from college basketball scouts. They came addressed to Mr. Elijah Thomas, printed on good paper with the college or university's letterhead at the top. Each week a new one would arrive, mixed in with his mother's bills, and he'd say the college or university's name out loud: University of Southern Mississippi. University of Michigan. Florida State. Syracuse. It was exciting, and he wanted to share the good news with his friends. What kept him from doing this, though, was the awareness that Dylan and Michael might not have the same opportunities, that their trajectories might be lower, limited to neighborhood jobs and living at home.

He didn't think Dylan minded, but Michael had big dreams

that included a fat bank account and expensive clothes. And a BMW 750, or whatever kind he was always talking about. What would happen if he didn't get those things? Elijah thought again about the guy in the hoodie and Michael's alleged *sponsor*. What if they were the same person? No, there was no way his friend would have done that to him.

In the ticket line, Michael thumped Elijah on the arm and said, "Hey, what's up with you?"

"Just thinking."

Michael screwed his face up to show that he didn't believe him. "Something's up, man. What is it?"

"Yeah," said Dylan. "What's your malfunction?"

"You really want to know?" Elijah affected a miserable expression, as though he were about to confide his deepest, darkest secret.

"Yes," said his friends together, drawing in close.

"I really wanted to hold hands with Dylan's mom."

Dylan jumped onto his back and pretended to wrap his friend up in a choke hold. Everyone laughed, even the other people in line, who were mostly other teenagers. Elijah took comfort in the fact that, for the moment, things were as they had always been.

THE NEXT MORNING, Elijah jogged to Banks's house and made it ten minutes early. He discovered a ten-foot mountain of sand in the middle of what had once been the driveway. Pallets of red concrete pavers were stacked beside it.

Elijah studied the situation. He'd want to stagger the joints of the pavers, but there was the question of whether to use straight or interlocking rows. He knocked on the front door to ask Banks.

"Morning, sunshine." Banks clenched an unlit cigar in his teeth.

Elijah took off his sneakers and followed him into the kitchen.

Instruction manuals were spread over what looked like a brand-new table and chairs. New, stainless steel appliances had been delivered, and the walls had been freshly painted.

"Whoa," said Elijah. "This place looks . . . nice."

"My daughter picked it all out. She's got her mother's good taste."

"Expensive?" Elijah touched something that might have been a cappuccino machine, or perhaps a juicer; he wasn't sure.

Banks shrugged. "Doesn't matter. There's not much to spend money on when you're a divorced guy in the army, except your kids."

"That's good of you." Elijah took one of the instruction manuals and flipped the pages until he found what he wanted. The diagrams showed how to arrange the pavers in an interlocking pattern. Another diagram showed pictures of the tools needed for the job. He folded up the manual and set it on the counter.

"I don't know about that; it's just how it is," Banks replied.

"My father never sent a penny. Not once." As soon as the words were out of Elijah's mouth, he realized that he'd broken his number one rule. He'd talked about his father. It was one thing for Elijah to think about him—another to disclose. But the words had slipped out so easily, unbidden.

"Neither did mine. I think today they call it being a deadbeat." Banks lit a new cigar off the oven's gas burner. "Funny— this appliance might be the most expensive cigar lighter in the world. I don't cook."

"Not at all?" asked Elijah.

"Never needed to. There was always a DFAC or O Club. What you'd call a cafeteria."

Elijah wondered how Banks had become such a hard case and if it had anything to do with his father. And if so, was Elijah at risk of becoming that way? He hoped not. Banks didn't seem like a bad guy, but he sure as hell wasn't much fun to be around. Still, if Elijah was going to continue working for him, he should try to get to know something about the man.

"Is your daughter still in high school?" asked Elijah.

Banks fixed his dark, suspicious eyes on him. "What's it to you?"

"Nothing. I'm just asking," said Elijah. "Making conversation."

Banks grunted. "Well, in case you haven't noticed, I'm not big on conversation."

"Nope, didn't notice. Because, you know, we've had so many great conversations, in between all the cigars and beers with lime juice, and the work."

Banks crossed his arms defensively. "Kerri's going to be here until the end of August. Then she leaves for college. In Manhattan. She's studying criminology, and then she wants to join the FBI. She's smart and beautiful and practical like her mother, who lives in Virginia and is a lawyer. Does that answer your question? Anything else?"

"What question?" Kerri walked into the kitchen; she was dressed but had a towel wrapped around her hair.

Banks scowled. "Nothing, sweetheart. We were talking about work."

"Right." Elijah tapped the folded-up instruction manual. "I'm going to need a shovel, a rake, and a tape measure. And some string, to keep the edges straight."

"I'll meet you outside." Banks brushed past Elijah and headed out the door.

But before Elijah could follow, Kerri stepped in front of him. "Did he give you the old 'keeping off the radar' speech?"

Elijah looked away uncertainly. "Yeah, he did. But I think he's just . . ."

"Out of his element is what he is." She tapped Elijah's arm with a pointed finger. "And just so you know, I'm not what you'd call *available*, but I'm no leper, either. So if you're up for a couple of lattes sometime . . . it might keep me from losing my mind around here. Know what I mean?"

"Uh, maybe." Elijah skirted past her and hurried for the door.

16

IT TOOK ELIJAH two hours to shovel the sand, and half as much time to spread it with the flat side of the rake. He tried not to think about Kerri, how she'd looked with her hair wrapped in a towel, and the graceful curve of her long, slender neck. She was beautiful, for sure, but that wasn't what distracted him. Rather, it was the way she carried herself. Smart and confident, yes, but there was something else. After all, how many girls did he know who were going to college in Manhattan to study criminology? And more important, what had she meant by "not available" but "no leper, either"? Was he supposed to ask her to go for coffee—or lattes, whatever exactly those were—or wait for her to ask?

Banks busied himself waxing and polishing his Jeep, which was a dark green Rubicon with oversized mud tires and a winch on the front bumper. When he finished, he lit up a cigar and watched Elijah work. "It's looking good." He took a green-and-gold medallion from his pocket and turned it in his hand absently.

"What's that?" asked Elijah.

"What?" Banks opened his hand and looked. "It's a challenge coin."

"Yeah, but what is it?"

"In the military, if a guy pulls off a difficult task, his commanding officer might give him one."

"Can I see it?" said Elijah.

Banks eyed him suspiciously but handed over the coin. It was about an inch and a half in diameter; the front had a yellow shield crossed by arrows, around which it said, "Special Forces Group" in raised letters. Below the shield were the words *de oppresso liber*. Elijah thought it was the coolest thing he'd ever seen. "What's the Latin mean?"

"Means the oppressed shall be liberated. It comes from an old poem by Saint Augustine. 'The needy have to be helped, the oppressed to be liberated, the good to be encouraged, the bad to be tolerated; all must be loved.'" Banks coughed into his fist. He looked embarrassed by his sudden lapse into poetry.

Elijah held the coin up, studying it. It seemed odd that an accountant would have a Special Forces challenge coin, but what did he know about the military? Maybe every division of the army had its own accountant. He knew that the military bought lots of things, so therefore it stood to reason that they needed to keep track of those purchases. Thus, accountants.

"If I ever joined the military," Elijah said, "do you think I could earn one of those?"

"Tell you what," said Banks. "You keep showing up on time and finish every job on the list, and that coin is yours."

"Really?"

"Sure, if you can do it." Banks took the coin and started back toward the house. "But I'm guessing one of these days you'll get a bug up your ass about something and stop showing."

"I won't," said Elijah. "You'll see." Because there was something about the medallion, the weight and feel of it, as well as the words and symbols cast in it, that had stirred feelings deep within him. Hope? Pride? Maybe he could join the military. And earn a bunch of coins with yellow shields, and Latin words that spoke of liberation from oppression, and love. He could be a part of something bigger than himself and know exactly where he belonged.

17

BONE-TIRED AND HUNGRY, Elijah put away the tools and grabbed his backpack, the outer pocket of which contained another envelope with a day's worth of pay. At the bottom of the driveway, he heard the quiet purr of the black Mercedes, followed by the zip of a power window.

"Get in," said the driver.

Elijah wanted to turn and run, but something primal and instinctive told him not to show fear. He opened the door and slid into the leather seat. A blast of chilled air hit his sweat-soaked T-shirt and made it feel like a solid, icy blanket. "How'd you know I'd be here?"

"Magician don't reveal his tricks, does he?"

"I guess not," said Elijah. "What do you want with me?"

"You're a long way from asking questions anytime you feel like it. How much do you know about me?"

"I don't know anything."

"You don't know facts, but you can guess." He steered the car with his left hand while unwrapping a green Jolly Rancher with the other. He popped it into his mouth and clicked it against his teeth. "Like on a test."

"You want me to try to figure out who you are?"

"Yeah. Go on and impress me."

Elijah took a deep breath before speaking. "You're driving an almost new Mercedes with nice aftermarket wheels, so you've got money and taste, but it's still a regular car. There are lots of them on the road, so it doesn't stand out too much. You've got standard plates, too, instead of custom or vanity ones. Those are too easy to remember, just like tattoos and jewelry, which you don't have, either. So you're not flashy, and you keep a low profile, which shows you're smart and disciplined, which in turn shows you're not like most of the losers who hustle around here."

He laughed, low and quiet. "That's good. I especially like the part about the other guys being losers. Always good to throw in some flattery; that never hurts. Anything else?"

"Yes, the most important thing: you're going to ask me to do something I don't want to do, which will leave me with the problem of saying no without disrespecting you."

"And you wouldn't want to disrespect me?"

"No."

"Because I have a gun?"

"For starters, yes. But this thing you want me to do, what if I can't do it?"

The Jolly Rancher clicked on the guy's teeth. "Listen. I got dudes lined up round the block waiting for a chance to conversate with me about business."

"I believe it." Elijah pointed out a right turn that would leave them several blocks short of his house, or Michael's. "Can you drop me over there?"

But the driver kept going straight, toward Michael's block. "Then you should believe that I ain't got time to hear what you want and what you don't want."

Elijah was silent. He didn't understand any of it, and yet there he was, surrounded by tan leather with polished wood inserts that probably weren't real wood but looked classy nonetheless. The dashboard glowed with Bluetooth and navigation programs, and hidden speakers pumped out a mellow hip-hop beat that Elijah liked in spite of himself.

"This is where one of your boys lives, right?" He pointed at Michael's brick and vinyl ranch.

"How do you know that?" said Elijah.

The driver waved a hand dismissively. "Easiest thing in the world to find out where people live. Not so easy to play ball like you do. So what we learned today is we both got valuable skills."

Elijah sat speechless next to the hooded figure. The Mercedes rolled to a stop in front of Michael's house.

"You can get out now," said the driver. "I'll let you know if you passed your test. Then we'll talk business."

Elijah got out but held the door open. "How about you tell me now and save the wait?"

But the car peeled away, nearly taking his hand with it as the force of acceleration slammed the door shut.

18

ELIJAH STOOD ON Michael's doorstep, trying to calm his nerves and look normal.

"Oh, hello, Elijah." Michael's youngest sister leaned her back against the wall, fluttering her eyelids. "Come on in and I'll get you a soda. What kind do you like?"

"Hi, Trisha," said Elijah. "I'm good. Thanks, though."

Trisha beamed as Michael shoved her out of the way. "I told you to stay in your room, Trisha. We got important stuff to talk about out here."

"What kind of stuff?"

"Man stuff."

"Ha! Ain't none of you men," chimed in Alexandria, who was only a year younger than Michael. "Though, Elijah does look good, his friendship with you notwithstanding." On the *you,* she poked Michael with a black-and-gold lacquered fingernail.

"What do you know about *notwithstanding*?" said Michael.

"More than you, stupid, because I pay attention in school," said Alexandria.

Michael's mother materialized from nowhere and stood between the two siblings. "Stop bickering at each other. You girls go on and give these boys some time. Then you can watch whatever you want."

"Bye, Elijah!" said Trisha as her sister pulled her toward their bedroom.

"Hey," said Dylan from his nest of overstuffed pillows on Michael's mother's couch. He balanced an iPad on his knees, watching YouTube videos from last year's Hoops. "You just got smoked by that dude who went on to play for Villanova."

"Donovan Murphy," said Michael.

"Yeah," said Dylan. "A fellow white brother."

"He smoked you, too, as I remember," said Elijah, pushing for space on the couch. "Dribbled right between your legs on his way to the winning layup." He was still rattled from his encounter in the Mercedes. He tried his best to sound normal.

"True enough," said Dylan. "I'm proud to get beat by him, though."

"Where you been?" asked Michael. "I finally get serious about practice, and you go missing."

"I've been working." *A half-truth,* thought Elijah.

Michael's mother called from the kitchen to ask if Elijah was hungry.

"Yes, ma'am. You know I never turn down your cooking." He felt too keyed-up to eat, but in Michael's house, there was only one rule: when his mother cooked, everyone ate, whether you were hungry or not.

Dylan paused the YouTube video and opened up a new tab. "Hey, what's the prize again if we win the whole tournament?"

"You know what it is," said Michael.

"I know, but I like hearing it. It never gets old. Go on, Elijah. Say it."

"Three thousand dollars," said Elijah. "Or a thousand each."

"That's so awesome," said Dylan. "Guess what I'm gonna buy with my share?"

"A real haircut?" said Elijah.

"Some clothes that fit you?" said Michael.

"My clothes are mad stylish. You two are just jealous of my style." Dylan turned the iPad around to show a full-screen image of a blond goddess in a string bikini. Airbrushed to perfection, she leaned over a yellow Mustang 5.0 convertible, showing ample cleavage. "Three hundred and fifty horsepower of pure driving pleasure," promised the ad.

"You're going to buy a make-believe woman?" said Elijah.

"No, stupid," said Dylan, clearly offended. "The car. My dream car. I'm gonna get me one."

Michael shook his head. "And he can buy one because a new 5.0 only cost a thousand dollars in Dylan's land of fantasy and make-believe."

"Shut up," said Dylan. "Don't you know what a down payment is?"

"Down payment." Elijah rolled his eyes, laughing.

"Here you go, Elijah," said Michael's mother, carrying a plate of stewed chicken thighs and potatoes, with greens on the side.

"Thank you, Mrs. Henderson."

"How about me?" said Michael. "You forget about your own son?"

Mrs. Henderson slapped Michael on the back of his head. "Your legs still work, right? And you're welcome, Elijah. How about you, Dylan? You want seconds?"

"Yes, ma'am," said Dylan.

When they finished eating, Michael's face lit up. "Okay, it's time."

"Time for what?" asked Dylan. "You're gonna sing for us? Remember when you sang that Michael Jackson song in the fifth-grade talent show?"

Dylan and Elijah cracked up, falling over each other on the

couch. It was rare for Michael to be the butt of the joke, which made it all the funnier.

"Man, shut up," said Michael. "Or I'll give your stuff away to someone who ain't ungrateful and stupid." Michael disappeared down the hallway and into his bedroom, then returned with a plain cardboard packing box.

"Is that what I think it is?" said Dylan, bouncing up and off the couch, grabbing at the box.

"Man, what's wrong with you?" said Michael, wrestling him back.

"I got ADD. You know that." Dylan struggled to free himself and have at the box again. "Let me see!"

"Your ADD's got ADD." Michael handed the box to Dylan, who tore it open and dug out three folded basketball jerseys. They were of serious quality, official NBA weight, the white body offset by green trim and orange letters that spelled out the team name, Elijah's Army. The color pattern perfectly matched their new Kobe 10s with the exception of a small circular patch. The patch showed a single drop of blood, like one half of the yin and yang symbol, only crimson. Next to the drop were the words *Street Nation* in black stylized script.

"This is our team's name?" said Elijah. "I like it, don't get me wrong. But this isn't my team, and we're definitely not an army."

"We are out there, on the court," said Michael. "Deal with it. You're the man. *El capitán.*"

"Whoa." Dylan held one up for all to see. He ran his fingers over the lettering, and then the Blood Street patch. "That's tight. What do you think, Elijah?"

Elijah shrugged, not trusting himself to speak. Wildly different emotions rose up and crashed inside him. On the one hand, the jerseys were amazing; he could picture himself and his teammates walking out onto the court in style. And he had to admit that the team name was a good one. But then there was that patch, and what it stood for—Blood Street Nation. It was so small and discreet, which, he supposed, was the genius of it. A tiny, little crimson icon that said so much, namely that he and his friends were about to play ball for a gang. A couple of weeks ago he'd have laughed at the possibility.

"It's great," said Elijah. "Really. I love it, except for the patch."

Michael placed one of his shovel-sized hands on Elijah's shoulder. "Look, man. Don't go bugging out about that patch, because it ain't nothing. I'm taking care of it."

"How? You're going to get rid of it?"

"I'm meeting with Money tomorrow, and we're going to work it out. I'm going to tell him how it is, and we're going to iron out the rules of his sponsorship."

Elijah said nothing.

"It's like this: Elijah's Army is all about ball, not business. BSN wants to set us up with a proper uniform, that's cool, but it ain't nothing more than that. Am I right, Dylan?"

"Yeah," said Dylan. "He's right. You know how ESPN's gonna film the quarterfinals, the semis, and the finals, right? And you know how there's gonna be college scouts watching. So it's good we got these jerseys, because me and Michael want you to look good out there. To get their attention."

"I appreciate that," said Elijah. "Really, I do. You two are the greatest friends a guy could have. But I'm really freaking nervous about being connected to a gang. Haven't we worked hard our whole lives to stay clear of that stuff?"

"You're right, but you got to trust me on this," said Michael. "I'm going to take care of it. I got a plan." And then, "Look, I didn't want to get into this, but for you two it's going to be strictly about ball. For me? Ball, and maybe a little business on the side."

"What kind of business?" Dylan spoke automatically, his eyes still fixed on the amazing Technicolor jerseys.

"I'll tell you some other time," said Michael. "Right now I

think you two should relax and let me do something good for you all. I mean, ain't I trying to take care of my friends?"

"Yes," said Dylan.

"Yes." Elijah wondered at what point, exactly, Michael had worn him down. Or was that an excuse? He wished he could talk it through with someone. Coach Walters, from his school team, would have been a good choice. But Coach spent summers traveling in his motor home. He made a point of telling his players that from June to August they should consider him missing in action. Which left Banks as the only other man he knew. Could he talk over something like this with Banks? Not if he expected any help, or even a polysyllabic response.

"That's right," said Michael. "And when we play, we're gonna win this joint and help get Elijah his shot at college ball. Come on and give me some love, my brothers!"

Elijah let himself be pulled in by his friends. They gave each other hearty whacks and thumps on the shoulders and arms. Maybe Michael was right, it was just about ball. Maybe the shoes and jerseys were gifts, with no strings attached. And maybe if he said it enough times, he'd actually believe it.

19

FOR THE FIRST TIME, Elijah automatically woke at six, before the buzz of his cell's alarm. He tried on his jersey and stood before the mirror. The team name looked especially good; from a distance, the patch resembled the small NBA logo, which gave him hope that not everyone would notice. But there was little chance of that, because up close, the patch practically glowed with the color of blood, a clear, strong indication that Elijah was in the deepest kind of shit. Trouble had found him at last, even though he'd maintained a 3.8 GPA and didn't get drunk, smoke weed, or fight (excepting the one altercation with Bull). Trouble in the form of a hundred-dollar tank top. He folded it and put it back into his dresser.

In the kitchen, his mother sat at the counter with a book and a cup of coffee. Elijah noticed how peaceful and content she looked; he wished her life could be easier, if only so she could have more times like this.

"Morning, stranger." She closed the book in her lap and smiled. "Are you going to work?"

"Uh-huh." Elijah lifted her mug and inspected the strong, black liquid. "More Turkish coffee?"

"Yes." She took it from him and sipped, trying not to make a face. "I'm developing a taste for it. How are things at Mr. Banks's house? Are you learning anything?"

"A little." Elijah filled a water bottle and grabbed an apple from the bowl on the counter. "But Banks isn't so good with tools and chores and things."

"Is that what you call him, Banks?"

"Yeah. He said he hates being called Mr. He said it's for guys with sticks up . . . Never mind." Elijah grabbed his backpack and keys. "I've got to go, Mom. I'll be back after work."

"Bye, Son. Say hello to . . . Banks for me."

THIRTY MINUTES LATER, Elijah filed in with a small crowd of early risers while a guard unlocked the front doors of the library. He walked briskly to the public access computers, where a librarian was booting up the terminals.

"It's my turn next," said a short man with an impossibly thick, reddish-brown beard. He wore Bermuda shorts and snow boots.

"That's cool," said Elijah. "I'm not going to take your turn."

The man looked up at him, his blue eyes blazing with manic intensity. He looked like he might go into attack mode, or possibly burst into tears. "Everybody takes my turn. They say they won't, but then they do."

"It's okay, man," said Elijah as calmly as possible. He remembered now why he never came to the public library; it was filled with crazy people. But it was also the only way he could research Blood Street Nation without his mother catching on. "I'm not going to take your turn. I swear."

The man stood for several seconds, blinking. "I don't want any trouble." Then he repeated it but more loudly.

"There is no trouble."

But the man turned and fled, the sound of his snow boots echoing off the linoleum tiles.

At an open computer terminal, Elijah Googled "Blood Street Nation" and came up with more than seven hundred hits. There was everything from Twitter feeds and Facebook posts to newspaper articles detailing crimes with suspected links to the gang. Stories of arson, murder, and drugs.

One feature in the *Baltimore Sun* was written by Dr. James Soldano. Of Blood Street Nation he said, "The gang is unique in three respects. First, relatively little is known about its history. However, it is believed to have originated in Los Angeles. Second, because of the decentralized power structure, Blood Street has been insulated from criminal prosecution; the few arrest to date have not led to significant conviction. And third, leaders have been described as virtually invisible, eschewing the notoriety and status typically enjoyed and prized by other leaders."

Elijah ran the cursor along each line of the article with growing dread. He continued reading: "The invisibility of Blood Street's leadership is its greatest strength. After all, how can you set up, catch, and prosecute those who don't have names or faces?"

Instantly he thought of the guy with the Mercedes, nameless and, thanks to his dark hood, almost faceless, too. Soldano's article closed with an 800 number for Baltimore's anti-gang task force. It was a generic plea for citizens to call in with any information about illegal gang activity; Elijah wrote the number on the inside of his hand, even though he suspected his problems were too big for Soldano and his task force. He logged out and raced to catch the seven o'clock bus that would take him to Banks's house.

20

ELIJAH FOUND BANKS in the side yard pouring gas into an old power mower. It was a Toro, the kind you'd find doing service in yards all across the country at this time of year. Except Banks's mower had been fitted with nylon straps and a forty-five-pound weight-lifting plate. Banks tested the straps to make sure they were secure.

"Good," he said. "You ready for the next job?"

Elijah walked around the machine, confused. "Why do you have weights on your lawn mower?"

"One weight. You can work up to two next week, if you can toughen up, that is."

"But why the weight?" said Elijah.

"Makes it work better." Banks grinned. "Greater traction."

Elijah tested the bar, but the Toro stayed put.

"Don't be afraid to put your back into it." Banks patted him on the shoulder and started to walk away. "When you're done, you can finish the driveway."

It took no fewer than ten pulls of the starter cord to get the old machine running. It turned over but rattled miserably as Elijah pushed and grunted it across the lawn. The front wheels dug into the soil, and he gritted his teeth as he put all his weight on the bar to free them. By the third pass, his calves, back, and shoulders burned from the tremendous effort needed to keep the mower moving.

"Hey," said Kerri, waving her right arm for him to stop. In her left she held a glass of iced tea.

Elijah shut off the mower and accepted the glass. "Thanks."

"You know," said Kerri, "it might work better without the heavy weight."

"Right."

"So maybe you should take it off."

"Right." Elijah returned the empty glass and pulled on the start cord again. "Thanks for the drink." The motor drowned out whatever Kerri tried to say in response.

AFTER MOWING THE LAWN, Elijah turned his attention to the driveway, which was exactly as he'd left it. He dropped a pile of pavers and began working each one individually, tapping it with a mallet until it matched its neighbor in depth and closeness. He liked that the materials were uniform, nothing more than concrete and sand. Aside from a few minor irregularities, like broken corners or humps in the underlying sand, there were no surprises. He only wished his life could be half as predictable.

"Not bad." Banks set one of his lime-beer concoctions on the remaining pallet of pavers. Elijah hadn't heard him come out of the house, but there he was, gray T-shirt, cigar, and all. "It looks almost professional."

"Thanks," said Elijah. "It'll look even better when I fill the gaps with sand. Then I'll need to tamp it really good. Do you have a tamper?"

"Never heard of it, but I can pick one up. I like the hardware store. It's a place of order and purpose. Know what I mean?"

"I guess so. I never thought about it before."

Banks drained the rest of his drink and fished car keys from a back pocket. "What's a tamper look like?"

"There's a picture of it in the instruction booklet. A piece of square steel with a wooden handle sticking out of the center." He studied Banks for a moment, wondering what about him was different. His graying beard stubble was back, but his eyes . . . they weren't so much cloudy as they were less intense. Muted. Elijah decided he was drunk. And what time was it—one o'clock? Two o'clock? Whichever, it was far too early to be sitting around your house drinking.

"I can drive," said Elijah.

"You're kidding, right?" Fire sparked in Banks's eyes. "It's one beer. You think you're my keeper just because my doctor tells me to take it easy? Is that what you think?"

"No," said Elijah, wondering what other craziness he'd stumble into before the day's end. First there had been the bearded guy at the library, and now a drunken, belligerent Banks. "I just want to drive your Jeep, that's all. I didn't think you'd let me, but you can't blame me for trying."

Banks considered for a moment. "Did Kerri put you up to this just now? Did she ask you to keep an eye on me?"

"No. I haven't talked to your daughter. Per your request, remember? She brought me a glass of iced tea and said hello. That was it."

Banks scowled. "Do you even have a license?"

"Permit. I can drive with a licensed adult."

Banks hesitated. "Okay, then." He tossed the keys high into the air.

THE MUD WHEELS and lift kit on the Jeep required that Elijah both step and pull himself up. He settled into the bucket seat and gripped the steering wheel. It was surprising how high he was, and he couldn't stop grinning.

"What are you smiling about?" said Banks. He looked uncomfortable in the passenger's seat, at least until he busied himself with the convertible top's release latch.

"Nothing. It's a nice truck. I like it." The inside of Banks's Jeep was all business: black vinyl seats; a flat, Spartan dash; and hand-crank windows. But every surface gleamed, and there wasn't a speck of dust. Elijah decided it was a real man's vehicle, one he far preferred to the flashy luxury of the black Mercedes. Elijah started the engine and shifted it into drive.

"If you mess it up . . . ," said Banks.

Elijah accidentally peeled out. "I won't."

"Go light on that pedal," said Banks. "There's three hundred and seventy-five horses under the hood. I custom-ordered this baby with an eight-cylinder power plant."

Banks continued talking about his beloved vehicle, the transmission's gearing and the particulars of the transfer case, but Elijah's concentration left little room for listening. "What?"

"I said I know why you really offered to drive."

"Yeah?"

"So what if I'm a little drunk. I'm retired. I'm not on active duty anymore, so I can do whatever the hell I want. Understand?"

"Yes." Elijah took a right-hand turn a little too quickly and felt the Jeep start to roll. "Whoa, sorry!" He corrected quickly, but Banks appeared not to notice. The man was busy rooting through his glove box, pulling out miscellany like the owner's manual, ketchup packets, and half a dozen lighters.

"Christ," said Banks. "No cigars. You know where West Ferry is? There's a smoke shop on the right, past the gas station."

Elijah leaned forward to study the street signs. He turned left on West Ferry and drove slowly, not recognizing a thing; it was a part of the city he'd never been to before. Block after block of rundown apartments, and small, independently owned shops instead of the ubiquitous franchises he was used to seeing.

"You ever been inside a cigar shop?" asked Banks.

"Nope."

"Come on. It's another place of order and purpose. A place that makes sense."

The outside of Carl's Tobacco wasn't much to look at: white painted cinder blocks covered by a flat roof. A pot of dead flowers was on the sidewalk next to a cast-iron kettle that was used as an ashtray. The front window was plastered with signs showing exotic names such as Arturo Fuente, Tres Reynas, and Pinar Del Rio. Inside, the walls were lined with shelf upon shelf of red cedar cigar boxes. The smell was terrific, even though Elijah was sure he'd never, under any circumstances, smoke a cigar.

Banks greeted the man at the counter, who was none other than Carl himself. Carl was almost as fat as he was tall, and was clad in a black-and-white-striped bowling shirt.

"Banks," said Carl. "What can I get you?"

"Macanudos. Maduro."

"How many?"

Banks held up three fingers, and Carl retrieved as many boxes from a glass case.

"Who's the kid?" said Carl.

"My driver," said Banks.

"I should have guessed you were famous enough to have a driver." Carl winked at Elijah and tossed him a pink cigar made of bubble gum. "Anything else?" he said to Banks.

"Nope. That'll do her. Onward, driver."

22

FROM WEST FERRY, Elijah followed Banks's directions through a maze of strip malls until he found the big-box hardware store on Patapsco Avenue. They walked past displays of rakes, shovels, and axes. Elijah finally picked out a wood-handled tamper priced at twenty dollars, and Banks paid with cash, a thick roll of twenties held together with a heavy brass clip. He spoke little, and communicated to the cashier mainly through nods. In the parking lot, he tossed the tamper into the backseat.

"You want to drive more?"

"Hell, yes," said Elijah, before adding, "Sir."

But Banks appeared not to hear him. He stared off into the far corner of the parking lot, even though it contained nothing of interest—pallets of roofing shingles covered in white plastic, and a fleet of black steel utility trailers.

Elijah watched Banks. He didn't understand what the man was doing, but knew not to interrupt. It wasn't a lapse of attention, or a daydream; rather it seemed as though he were somewhere else. His ramrod posture sagged under some kind of invisible weight, until, all at once, he snapped out of it and turned toward the Jeep.

"What are you looking at?" he said. "Didn't your mother teach you not to stare?"

"No—I mean, nothing. I'm just waiting." Elijah kept his hand on the driver's door, hopeful that he'd get another shot at driving. He didn't know what Banks's malfunction was, nor did he especially care. He had problems of his own, and at the moment, all he wanted to do was get back behind the wheel.

Banks shook his head vigorously. "I'm sorry. I've got some things on my mind."

"Me too," said Elijah.

"No kidding." Banks looked intently at him. "I thought it was supposed to be all fun and games at your age."

"It's supposed to be," said Elijah. "Isn't, though. At least, not right now, but I don't want to talk about it."

"Good." Banks went back to watching the piles of roofing shingles. "Neither do I."

"So where to next?"

"Hungry?" said Banks.

"I'm starving," said Elijah.

Banks tossed him the keys. "Cheeseburgers. Cherry Hill Road." He directed Elijah through a series of zigzags around unfamiliar streets, where burned-out buildings and abandoned crack houses proliferated among graffiti-tagged convenience stores advertising lotto tickets and cheap cigarettes. At intersections, homeless people pushed shopping carts filled with empty cans, towering piles that threatened to spill out at any moment.

Outside the storefronts, young men in ball caps and hoodies glared hard at Elijah. Their looks said, *Get out of that Jeep and I'll mess you up.* He was reminded again of the crazy little man from the library who didn't want any trouble. *Me neither,* he thought.

"Up ahead," said Banks.

"Up ahead where?" asked Elijah.

"That little place on the right," said Banks. "They serve good food. I grew up around here, if you can believe it. It was never a great place, but now . . ." He shook his head. "Bums and addicts. Half these men are in their twenties. Do you mean to tell me that they can't work? That, physically, they're incapable of showing up somewhere on time and doing something useful?"

"I don't know." Elijah parked the Jeep on the street, and they entered a small, aluminum-sided diner with a row of booths against the outer wall. A red Formica counter separated the customers from the kitchen, which consisted of a pair of grills and fryers manned by a slow-moving old man in a paper chef's hat. Banks and Elijah claimed stools between a pair of surly-looking old-timers wearing caps embroidered with military insignia. They all nodded to Banks, but it was impossible to tell whether they knew each other or were simply being polite.

"What do you boys want?" said the waitress, a short curvy woman with a name tag that said "Sherita."

"Bacon double cheeseburger," said Banks, "regular fries, and a Coke."

Sherita lowered her eyes in Elijah's direction. "And you, handsome?"

He turned to Banks. "Are you buying?"

"Yeah," said Banks. "You earned a good meal. Knock yourself out."

"In that case, I'll have a cheeseburger, curly fries, a Coke, and a large milk shake. Chocolate, please."

"Well, ain't he polite," said Sherita. And then, to Banks, "You could try being polite sometime. It wouldn't hurt you."

Banks accepted the teasing with a smile but kept quiet.

The guy next to Banks nudged him, "How's retirement, chief?"

"Like watching paint dry," said Banks.

"Oh, it's not so bad," said the guy. "What you need to do is get yourself a routine. That's what I did."

Banks made a low grunting noise that the guy took for encouragement.

"Oh, I go for breakfast at the McDonald's on Fairmont with a bunch of other guys every Monday, Wednesday, and Friday. They give us the senior discount *and* the veteran's discount, you know. Then at ten o'clock I go over to the off-track betting on Springville Road. I bet five dollars and watch the horses, and then I go home for a nap. But that's just the morning part; I got a whole 'nother routine for the afternoon, and a different one for weekends, too."

"Huh," said Banks. "You just talked me into reenlisting."

A couple of the other guys laughed, and Sherita slid plates in front of Banks and Elijah, piled high with half-pound burgers and french fries.

"Here you go, boys," she said. "Enjoy."

Elijah inhaled his food, pausing only to breathe, and then again to tell Sherita how good it tasted.

Banks ate methodically, with a level of seriousness and precision that one might reserve for filling out tax forms or defusing a bomb. Halfway through, he doused everything with ketchup, mustard, and Tabasco sauce.

"You don't like it?" asked Elijah.

"It's good. In the army we drown everything like this. Habit."

"Do you miss it? Being in the army?" Elijah's plate was clean. He peeled the paper off his straw and started in on his milk shake.

"Nah," said Banks. "But maybe I got used to it. And I was good at it. There were rules for everything, and if you followed them, you got results. I liked that part."

"Predictable," offered Elijah, hoping to keep the conversation going. He had to admit that, despite Banks's surliness, he was kind of interesting. After all, what did Elijah know about him, other than the few pieces of information the man had shared? Practically nothing.

"Civilian life makes no sense—smart phones, metal detectors in schools, six-dollar cups of coffee with soy milk and caramel drizzled on top. And all that hip-hop gang shit."

"There are no hip-hop gangs, you know. They're two separate things, though many gang members do listen to hip-hop."

"That right?"

"It is, although the opposite isn't always true. Not everyone who listens to hip-hop is in a gang."

"I'll keep all that in mind." Banks lowered his head and resumed eating.

Elijah tried to imagine a younger Banks in uniform doing army things. In his mind he saw canvas tents and corrugated metal buildings. And inside one of them sat Banks at a desk, ramrod straight, dark eyes blazing with disapproval.

When he finished eating, Banks pushed his plate away and laid down a twenty and a ten.

"You need change, honey?" said Sherita.

"Keep it." Banks turned and shook hands with the old-timers.

"Now, ain't you the big spender," said Sherita, head cocked to the side, one hand on her hip.

"My version of politeness," said Banks. "Is it acceptable?"

"Any day of the week, sugar," said Sherita.

23

"SHE LIKED YOU," said Elijah on their way out the front door.

"She liked the tip," said Banks. "Nothing wrong with that, but it's a different kind of like. Hell, maybe it's more honest."

"She called you sugar. Sugar means she likes you."

"Is that so? You know about all sorts of things: hip-hop gangs and waitresses."

"That's right," said Elijah. "I do, and you're lucky to have me driving you around and interpreting local culture. You'd be lost otherwise."

"You're probably right," admitted Banks. "I could have used an interpreter of local culture fifteen years ago; maybe I'd still be married."

Elijah noticed a chubby young man in a black-and-gold track-suit standing a little too close to Banks's Jeep. He had wedged one of his Timberlands between the tubular running board and the doorframe, giving him enough purchase to lean inside and examine the steering column.

Another guy stood watch. He was the same height as Banks but had grotesquely veined muscles that bulged out of a red, white, and blue Wizards tank. "Yo." He raised his hand at chest level. "My man, hold up!"

Banks regarded him coolly. "What's up, young blood?"

"Not much, old man." Wizards Tank drew his hand back. "This your ride?"

"Yeah," said Banks. "What's it to you?"

Oh shit, thought Elijah. *This isn't going to end well.* His heart began to pound. He looked up and down the street, but there were no cops in sight. Worse, the people on the street seemed to sense trouble; they had disappeared back into their apartments and bodegas.

The muscle guy opened his arms in an expansive gesture that revealed gang tattoos scribed along his inner biceps. "Me and my associate were doing you a favor, see. Because this is what you might call a high-crime neighborhood, we was—"

"Get to the point," said Banks, making a small circle with his finger. He fished keys from his back pocket and, to Elijah's horror, jingled them in front of the guy like bait.

"We was protecting your car from thiefs while you and your boy ate dinner."

Elijah felt a twinge of something deep inside. *You and your boy.* He hated how powerful the suggestion of that relationship was to him, and now he had to wait for Banks to correct it. *He's not my boy. Elijah's nobody's boy. He doesn't even know who his father is.* But Banks let it pass.

"How much for your services?" Banks asked.

The guy seemed taken aback, confused at how unafraid Banks seemed to be. And by how quickly Banks had become the one asking the questions. "Well, ordinarily we charge fitty. But for you . . ."

For a second, it looked like Banks was reaching for his wallet. But then his body sprang into motion in a completely unanticipated way. Without so much as a twitch, the inner blade of his hand shot out and drove into the guy's Adam's apple. The heavily muscled man dropped to his knees, hands clutching at his throat as his eyes bugged out in surprise.

Banks knelt down and slipped the guy's wallet from his front pocket. He fished out a driver's license and tossed the wallet at the kneeling man's head. Only then did he stalk toward the driver's-side door and the guy in the tracksuit.

"Wait," said Tracksuit, backing away with his palms up.

"I'm doing your friend a favor," said Banks, waving the ID. "Because this is a high-crime neighborhood, I'll keep this safe until tomorrow, and then he can buy it back from me. What do you think is a fair price, fifty bucks?"

"I don't know, mister," said Tracksuit. "I don't want any trouble."

"Too late for that, fat boy," said Banks. "Because I already crushed your friend's windpipe. Tell me, can you run fast in that fancy suit?"

"What?" He glanced at his associate, who was still making terrible choking noises. "I don't know what you're talking about, mister."

"I want to see your fat ass run. I'll give you a head start." Banks looked at his watch and started counting down. "Five. Four."

The guy stared, disbelieving.

Banks looked up from his watch and took a step toward the guy. "Three. Two."

Before Banks hit one, Tracksuit turned and bolted, his chubby, velvet-covered arms pumping for speed.

"Not bad." Banks tossed the keys to Elijah and pulled himself up and into his Jeep. "Let's go, driver."

24

ON THE ROAD, Banks fished one of his new Macanudo cigars from one of the boxes he'd purchased from Carl. Inside was a cheap cutter, which he used to trim the end.

Elijah backtracked through the unfamiliar streets, trying to remember the way. When he couldn't stand the quiet any longer, he said, "Okay, I've got to know. How did you do that?"

"I punched him in the throat." Banks puffed his cigar alive. He held it out for inspection (or maybe appreciation) and then put it back into his mouth. "There's not a whole lot to it."

"I know," said Elijah. "But how did you *do* that . . . you know, handle the situation? That was . . . that was awesome."

"It's the law of inevitables."

"The law of what?"

"The law of inevitables. If the circumstances demand action, then it's best to act immediately. Without deliberating."

"What if . . ."

"There's no what ifs. Remember this, Elijah: if you're in a bad situation and the only advantage you have is to act quickly, with surprise, then that's what you've got to do. Thinking and weighing the odds just gets in the way."

Elijah thought back to his altercation with Bull. He'd known

Bull was going to beat his ass. But with the guy in the Mercedes, he couldn't predict what he was going to say or do. The situation did not demand action—at least, not yet.

"Can I ask you something?" said Elijah.

"What."

"How did you learn all that? I mean, I thought you said you were an accountant. Accountants don't beat up giant street thugs."

"Army accountants are tougher than the ones at H&R Block." Banks flashed a rare grin. "Listen, I'm supposed to be taking it easy, if you know what I mean."

"Not really."

"Physically, I'm supposed to be taking it easy. As in avoiding stress. It's why I told your mother I could use some help around the house when she first asked me."

Elijah nodded, still unclear.

"So it's probably best if Kerri doesn't know about our little adventure with the world's dumbest car thieves. All right?"

"Got it," said Elijah, already relishing the idea of the secret. "Just a boring dinner with some old retired guys."

"Right." Banks grinned around the stub of his cigar.

Elijah parked the car in front of Banks's house but kept the Jeep running. "Can I ask you something? A couple of things, actually."

"What?" said Banks.

"First, I need two days off because I'm playing in a basketball tournament."

"And the second thing?"

"If you know any more things like the law of inevitables, could you teach me?"

"We'll see."

THAT EVENING, Dylan's mother drove the boys to the mall in her tiny Honda Civic hatchback. Elijah and Michael rode in the backseat with their knees crushed into their chests. They discussed their strategy for the tournament while Dylan and his mother talked about family business, trying to arrange their next visit to prison to see Dylan's brother, Marvin.

At the mall's front entrance, Elijah and Michael grunted and groaned as they extricated themselves from the backseat. Mrs. Buchanan tried to hand Dylan a twenty-dollar bill. "Buy your friends a pizza."

"No thanks, Mom." Dylan pushed it away and kissed his mother on her cheek. "Save it for gas for the trip. Brothers before pizza. Besides, we've got money."

"Do you boys need a ride home? I can run some errands and come back."

"No thanks, Mrs. Buchanan," said Elijah. "We'll catch the bus."

"Thanks for the ride," said Michael.

Inside, they wandered through the two sporting goods stores, examining shoes, clothes, and sweats, all of which cost far too much.

"These." Dylan stopped at a pair of white basketball shorts with orange stripes. "They match the shoes."

Elijah flipped the price tag. "Fifty bucks!"

"Come on, guys," said Dylan, holding them up for display. "They're perfect."

"Do you even have fifty bucks?" asked Michael.

"No, but you don't have to be all negative." Dylan put the shorts back, and they eventually settled on a plain white pair at an even ten bucks.

"They're not as nice," lamented Dylan over a sweet-and-sour-chicken combo platter from the food court.

"You can buy the nice ones after we win," said Michael between forkfuls of sausage lasagna. "Elijah, how many pairs of them shorts can homeboy get with a thousand dollars?"

"Twenty pairs," said Elijah. "And if he changes them every three days, he can get through most of the year without doing laundry."

"Funny." Dylan had finished his Chinese food and was eying Elijah's slices of deep-dish pizza. "You going to eat that second piece?"

"Touch it, and you will pull back a bloody stump." Elijah slid his tray farther away.

"Hey," said Michael, rapping the side of Elijah's head with his knuckles. "See that girl over there? She's waving at me. Watch this. I'm going to talk her up."

Elijah spotted Banks's daughter three tables away, sitting by herself with a book. He put a hand on Michael's arm. "Sorry, Casanova, but she's not waving at you. I got this."

26

ELIJAH WASN'T ESPECIALLY nervous around girls, but there was clearly something unusual about Banks's daughter. For one thing, she was by herself with a book, instead of sitting in a protective circle of pretty friends. And she didn't look like the girls in his school; it wasn't so much the way she wore her clothes and hair as how she held herself. Composed. Assured, he decided. And then there was the matter of growing up with Banks as a father, which would have been enough to make anyone stand apart.

"I almost didn't recognize you without concrete dust stuck to your sweat," she said.

"That was just spray-on." Elijah took a seat across from her at the tiny metal table. "For effect." He looked back once and saw Dylan making a big show of eating his last slice of pizza. "Your father would have a major fit if he knew I was talking to you."

"Probably." Kerri marked her place in the book and set it on the table. "But I'm a big girl; I can decide for myself who I want to talk to."

Elijah took this as a positive sign, but he had no clue what to say next. "Your father said you're going to college somewhere in Manhattan?"

"The old 'where do you go to school' question," she said. "You can do better than that."

"Sure," said Elijah, feeling a line of sweat standing out on his brow. "How about this: How did you turn out so . . . normal, with Banks as a father?"

"I'm not normal." Her answer came quickly, as though she were stating a simple fact. "I study criminology all day. In my free time, I read books about murderers." As proof, she held up her book, the title of which was *In Cold Blood,* by Truman Capote.

"Yes, but you're not chewing on a cigar. You haven't grunted once. And your style goes so far beyond the plain gray T-shirt."

"You're funny." She laughed. "I wouldn't have guessed that."

"Why not?" said Elijah.

"I don't know. Six-foot-four jock covered in concrete dust. But since you brought up the subject of my father, maybe you can tell me what you two did yesterday when you *allegedly* went to the diner."

"What do you mean 'allegedly'?" Elijah remembered Banks's caution and registered his disappointment; she was talking to him only to find out about her father.

"Um, I'll ask the questions here, thank you very much." Her smile was broad and sincere, not at all like her father's crooked facsimile. "Let me put it another way. Did my father instigate any arguments or fights? Or interrogations?"

Elijah resisted the urge to smile, because it hadn't been at all like a fight. Fights involved two people hitting each other; what had happened with Banks had been more like a surprise attack. Crippling and completely effective.

"We went to Home Depot to buy a tool," he said. "Then we went for burgers in the bad part of town and ate at the counter with a bunch of old retired guys. That's it. Oh, and the waitress's name was Sherita."

"Yes, that's the official version I got, but I'm not convinced. I think you two got into some kind of trouble." Kerri pushed her glasses up onto her hair and studied him. "All I know is that when he came back, he was different. Not himself."

"What was wrong?"

"Nothing was wrong; that's the problem. He's usually grumpy and unpleasant to be around."

"And he wasn't?"

"No. He was, like, excited. We stayed up late talking, which never happens . . . because he never wants to talk. Plus, he didn't drink or smoke himself to sleep."

"Maybe he did but in secret. How would you know?"

"I'm the one who empties his ashtrays and puts all the beer bottles into the recycling bin. I did it when I was little, too, before my parents divorced. Lots of practice, you could say."

"You do know it's not a crime to be happy."

"Um, have you met my father? Mr. Grizzled Hard-Core Military Guy? For him it is a crime. The order of people who are sure to go to hell is like this: axe murderers, arsonists, pedophiles, slackers, and then happy people."

Elijah smiled. "Yeah. Actually, I have met that guy. I thought he just had a grudge against me."

"He's that way with everyone."

Elijah felt the eyes of his idiot friends watching him from the other table. Any minute they would come over to embarrass him. *Keep talking,* he told himself. "You know, I still can't picture him as an accountant. It doesn't fit."

"Are you changing the subject? Because I still think you're lying. I think you two had some kind of, I don't know, adventure or something. Did he take you to a shooting range? Jumping out of an airplane? Come on, tell me what you two really did."

"You just met me and you're calling me a liar."

"Well?"

"We went to a diner. We ordered cheeseburgers. I got curly fries and he had regular ones. He told me that his were preferable because they were efficient to eat. More functional, he said. Who talks that way?"

She grinned.

"How could I make something like that up? I'm not that creative."

"Well . . . that does sound like something he'd say." Satisfied, Kerri snapped up her book and stood. "Nice talking to you. I've got to go."

"That's it? Where are you going?"

"See you later, Basketball Player."

"Wait." But he was talking to her back. "I still don't know anything about you."

Kerri turned her head. "That's right. You don't. And the statute of limitations on lattes expires in two days." She disappeared into the dense, moving mass of shoppers, and Elijah returned to his friends.

"ALL RIGHT," SAID MICHAEL. "Hot new girl. Who is she, and when are you going to introduce me?"

"Do you think I'm crazy? I'm not going to introduce you," said Elijah. "She's smart and beautiful. You're a pig."

"That hurts," said Michael. "It's petty and cruel, but I respect your fear of my sexual powerfulness. I wouldn't introduce me, either."

"That's not a word, *powerfulness.*"

"It should be," said Michael. "I ain't responsible for the inadequacies of the language."

"*Inadequacies is* a word," said Elijah. "Much better!"

"Okay, professor," said Michael. "But seriously, who is she?"

"Her name's Kerri. She's the daughter of that guy I'm doing yard work for."

"The retired dude? Damn, I might have to do me some yard work, if you know what I'm talking about."

"No. What *are* you talking about?" said Dylan.

"You'd have to actually do some work," said Elijah. "That's a deal breaker for a major player like you, right?"

"Probably," said Michael. "Are you talking about real hard work? Like with shovels and wheelbarrows and stuff?"

The boys dumped their trays and walked outside to the bus stop. Dylan had brought his ball, and they passed it around as they waited. It went back and forth, changing directions, and threading through legs and behind backs. The speed of passing increased until the ball became a blur, distinguished only by the hands that were passing from the ones receiving. They continued to talk and horse around, but the ball never stopped moving. When their bus arrived, they stashed the ball and sat close.

"Tournament starts in less than fourteen hours," said Elijah. "Are we still meeting tomorrow morning at your place?"

"You know it," said Michael. "Our moms are making us food."

"Hey," said Dylan. "I'm nervous. I might be up all night. Going to watch *Coach Carter*, *Above the Rim*, and *Love & Basketball*. Get me inspired."

"You should watch *Space Jam*," said Elijah. "That's more your speed."

"Maybe I will," said Dylan. "Michael Jordan, baby!"

At their stop, the boys bumped fists and went their separate ways home.

28

ELIJAH WAS NOT surprised to find the black Mercedes parked in front of his mother's house. He stalked to the passenger door, opened it, and got in. This time, the man in the driver's seat wasn't wearing a hood. His head was shaved. Early twenties, with light coffee-colored skin, and a hard, chiseled face. Not the friendliest-looking guy, but not overtly evil-looking, either.

A flick of the finger activated the door locks. "Big day tomorrow."

"Yeah."

"You're going to play in front of all them people and represent. That means you and me, we're connected now."

"How's that? I don't even know your name."

"You need me to spell it out? I thought you were smart. I thought you'd put two and two together."

"I can add," said Elijah. "But I want to hear it from you."

"Name's Money. And from now on, Blood Street Nation's your family."

"I've got a family."

Money sucked his teeth. "You should be honored. We only take the best."

Elijah paused to let it sink in.

Money thumped him hard on the shoulder. "Smile, dawg. This is a good thing."

"Exactly who is the Nation?" said Elijah.

"For now it's you and your boys. One small, tight unit. Like a little military unit. That's why the boss came up with the name Elijah's Army."

"What are we supposed to do?"

"Play ball and represent. Win Hoops. After that, we'll talk. But one step at a time, baby."

"What if we don't win?"

"Don't be asking what-ifs. Just do your job, like a good soldier." Money held out his fist for a bump.

Slowly, reluctantly, Elijah touched his knuckles to Money's. He looked out the window at his house; the living room light was still on. He knew his mother was waiting up for him, probably beginning to worry. It would break her heart if she knew the choice he was making. How could he explain it to her? Could he say he was doing it to protect her? That he'd let Michael pressure him? No, he couldn't put it off on other people. He was the one bumping fists with this person, Money. He was choosing, and he would have to pay the price.

"Okay, but tell me what's next," said Elijah. "After basketball."

"Life. Business. You and your boys work hard and prove yourselves. Make some green. You ain't got a problem with the green, do you?"

"No," said Elijah. "But I've got a job."

"Mowing lawns ain't a job; it's a waste of time and talent. Listen, if you're half as smart as the boss thinks, you gonna be driving a Mercedes, too."

"Who's the boss?"

"You'll know that when you prove yourself, which you can start doing at Hoops."

"What if I don't want a Mercedes?"

"Then a BMW. Lexus. Whatever."

"What I mean," said Elijah, bracing himself for the return of the silver handgun, "is what if I don't want to be a part of the Nation?"

Another grin, this one colder. "Everybody wants to be part of the Nation, baby. We're small, exclusive, and all-powerful. Nobody knows who the boss is, not even the cops. But here's the straight answer: it don't matter what you want. You're wearing the Blood tomorrow, and that makes you one of us."

"You mean that little patch? That doesn't mean anything."

Money's sharp face turned toward him, slitted eyes reading him, studying him, like a snake ready to strike. His voice was low and smooth, no longer discussing or explaining. He was stating facts.

"The Nation owns you, baby. Everybody got their price, and you know what yours is?"

"No," Elijah lied. He wanted to plug his ears and go back in time, to before things had gotten so complicated.

"Your price is a pair of shoes." Money hit the button that unlocked the doors, a signal that their time was up. "But don't feel bad about that; most people cost less. Now get out of the car and win me a goddamned trophy."

SLEEP DID NOT come easily that night for Elijah. At twelve o'clock, he gave up and called Michael's cell.

After a sample from R. Kelly's "I'm a Flirt" came the following instructions: "Fine ladies can leave a message; everyone else, I'll catch up with you later."

"Can't sleep," said Elijah after the beep. "Call if you're up, because I was thinking about walking to Joe's. And you really need to change that message!"

Thirty seconds later, his phone rang.

"Joe's?" said Michael.

"Yeah. I'm craving a hot dog and cheese fries."

"If you're buying, sure."

"Who said anything about buying? I'll be at your house in five."

The air had cooled enough to be pleasant, and they sat at a picnic table outside Joe's Texas Hots, which was the only all-night restaurant in their neighborhood. It also happened to be dirt cheap. They ordered foot-long hot dogs, cheese fries, and large Cokes. Michael swatted at a seagull that hovered at a safe distance, poaching stray fries.

"I hate those things," he said. "They're nasty." He tented a napkin over his fries and stood up.

"What are you doing?" asked Elijah.

"Gotta go to the bathroom." He pointed at his food. "This is so none of them flying rats will eat my fries."

Elijah shrugged and took a bite of his hot dog. On the sidewalk, a muscular guy carrying a gym bag walked by. The guy looked in his direction, squinting. Elijah tried to figure out where he recognized him from. School? No, too old for high school. The Battlegrounds? Maybe. He sipped his Coke and then he remembered—Bull.

The big man came closer, separated by only a row of planter boxes. The gold ring in his nostril flared with each enraged breath. "You tell Money he's a dead man. You tell him I'm—"

Elijah dropped his hot dog and put his hands up. "Hang on. I don't know what you're talking about."

Bull jabbed a finger into the space between them. "I seen you with Money. At the Battlegrounds parking lot."

"So what?"

Bull's face twitched. "I heard one of Money's boys shot my nephew."

"I'm not Money's boy," said Elijah. "I swear. You want to come at me because I hit you, fine. But I didn't shoot anybody. I've never even held a gun."

Bull scowled. Thinking. Deciding.

Keep talking, thought Elijah. Out of the corner of his eye he saw Michael returning from his phone call, closing the distance with long, silent strides. "Who's your nephew?"

"Ray Shiver."

"I knew him. He was in my AP English class. I'm sorry, really."

"Yeah, AP classes," said Bull. "That was Ray. You smart too?"

"I guess so," said Elijah.

"Good." A cruel line of a smile spread across his face. "Then you'll understand why I gotta do this." He stepped over the planter boxes and toward Elijah, just as Michael wedged himself between the two of them.

"Back off," said Michael, chest to chest, eyes locked. "How come you look like you're about to jump my boy Elijah?"

Elijah managed to get his long legs out from under the picnic table, expecting blows at any minute, but they didn't come.

"Ask him." Bull's face was a mask of rage and frustration. He looked from Michael to Elijah, and then back to Michael.

"I'm asking you," Michael said.

"He sucker punched me," said Bull.

Michael raised an eyebrow.

"I hit him," said Elijah. "But just once."

"Now I'm gonna hit you." Bull tried to muscle his way past Michael, until a crack in the background stopped them all. Harold, a cook who used to play ball at the Battlegrounds, had slammed the back kitchen door against its frame. He stood, tall and furious in his white apron, pointing his spatula at Bull.

"Man, get the hell outta my restaurant," he said.

"This ain't *your* restaurant," said Bull.

"It is when I'm cooking," said Harold.

"It's a public place," said Bull. "I can be here as long as I want."

"You can until Louie comes out here and eighty-sixes you for bothering customers. You wanna go the rest of the year with no more hot dogs or french fries?"

Bull looked at the two boys, clearly deliberating between revenge and continued access to the best hot dogs in town. "I'm going," he said at last, "but this ain't over."

After the big man was out of earshot, Michael said, "Why do you have a beef with him? You don't ever fight."

"He kept fouling me on the court, so I punched him in the nuts. Listen, Michael. Thanks—"

Michael cut him off with a hand. "Forget it. You want to thank somebody?" He pointed at Harold. "That's the man."

"Harold," said Elijah, walking over to shake hands. "I owe you. Big-time."

"Forget it," said Harold. "That dude's an animal. But you know he's gonna keep coming after you, right?"

Elijah nodded.

Harold cupped a hand over his mouth for privacy, even though they were the only ones on the patio. "If you want to get a piece for protection, I can hook you up."

"We're okay," said Elijah. "Thanks, though."

"It's cool," said Harold. "I'm just saying."

And because the seagulls had eaten their food, Harold packed a bag for them, which they carried home and ate on Elijah's front stoop. The concrete still held some of the day's heat, and it was quiet and comfortable.

"How come you didn't tell me you mixed it up with Bull?" asked Michael in between bites of his second foot-long.

"Honestly? I was proud of myself for handling it all on my own."

"Sounds like you *did* handle it," said Michael. "Shit just comes back around, though, don't it?"

"Yeah. But you were right there to back me up. Thanks, man," said Elijah.

"No problem. I *always* got your back. You know that."

"I do," said Elijah. "I really appreciate it."

"Shit. That's what brothers are for. You still worried about them jerseys?"

"Forget it. Let's just focus on the tournament and making it through to the finals."

30

THE BOYS MET early at Michael's house, their spectacular uniforms concealed beneath plain gray sweats. Elijah's mother was busy in the kitchen with Michael's and Dylan's mothers, preparing snacks: sandwiches, bananas, granola bars, and plenty of Gatorade, kept cold in an Igloo cooler filled with ice.

"Picture time," said Dylan's mother. "You boys get close together. Smile for real, none of those pinched, fake ones."

They posed in front of the door, Michael in the center with his million-dollar grin, flanked by his two best friends. Their arms hung loosely over each other's shoulders. At the pop of the flash, Elijah wondered if they'd look different at the end of the tournament. Could they really compete in the adult division, against college guys, hard-core street ballers, and trash talkers with more muscle and body ink than skill? They would, because they had to.

Elijah's mother pulled him down to her level so she could kiss his cheek. "Have fun and don't get hurt. I'll be in the stands watching."

"Okay, Mom," he said. "I love you."

* * *

111

THEY ARRIVED AT the Battlegrounds fifteen minutes early, feeling loose and warmed up. The surrounding blocks were closed off to traffic, and close to two thousand people were packed into every conceivable space. Food carts sold everything from pizza and hot dogs to Greek and Thai. Other vendors sold T-shirts, baseball caps, and even sneakers.

It took them a few minutes to navigate through the crowds and find the registration table. They peeled off their sweats and waited in line behind another team.

"How come everybody's looking at us?" asked Dylan.

"Because we look good," said Michael.

At the table, a guy in a T-shirt that said "Volunteer" scrutinized their IDs. "You boys aren't old enough for the adult division."

"It's okay," said Michael. "We automatically qualified because of our standing in the eighteen-and-under division last year."

"Yes," said Dylan. "And here's our parent permission forms, and a letter from our high school coach."

The volunteer checked the coach's signature. "You boys play for Bernie Walters? Why didn't you say so? He told me he had some real players this year." He shuffled the papers into a stack and set them aside. "What's your team name?"

"Elijah's Army," said Dylan with obvious pride.

The volunteer wrote down their name and handed them each a blue plastic bracelet that fastened with an adhesive strip. "Okay, guys. Make sure you keep your bracelet on until the tournament is over. If you take it off or attempt to transfer it to another player, your team will be immediately disqualified."

"Yes, sir," said Dylan.

"We've got a strong field of competition this year, boys. You'll be playing against teams from Atlanta, Richmond, and DC. And remember, it's single elimination. Are you ready?"

They nodded.

A different volunteer pointed to several giant dry-erase boards affixed to the fence. "At any of the boards," he explained, "Elijah's Army will be listed as the very last team, number sixteen. Go on over, find that number, and you can see who you'll be playing. Games begin in twenty minutes. Good luck."

"Thanks," they all said.

The meager patch of grass and gravel surrounding the Battle-grounds was a mob scene. Several TV crews worked the crowd, interviewing players and fans indiscriminately. The boys maneuvered through the people and stood before one of the big dry-erase boards.

"There." Dylan pointed at the first bracket of games. "That's us, team sixteen."

31

"IT SAYS WE'RE playing team number seven," said Michael. "B City Shooters. Court two. You guys heard of them?"

Elijah and Dylan shook their heads. Games were under way on six of the Battlegrounds' eight courts. Fans pressed up against the fences watching, cheering, and booing. The boys walked past Jones, who was still in his spot under the live oak tree, presumably giving odds and taking bets. He was wearing his banker's hat and another one of his crazy T-shirts. This one said "Naturally Fly."

"Elijah's Army," said Jones. "Looking good. I'm giving you boys favorable odds this morning. Don't let me down."

They slapped hands with the bookie as they walked by; Michael stayed back and exchanged some private words with him. They shook hands, both grinning broadly.

"What was that about?" asked Elijah when Michael caught up.

"Just placing a little bet," said Michael.

Court two was ringed with a smaller, quieter assortment of fans. Michael threw his arms around his friends' necks and pulled them in close. "You see that dude?" He motioned with his eyes toward a guy in an orange polo shirt.

"Which one?" said Dylan.

"The one with the thermos and the notebook?" asked Elijah.

"Yeah, him," said Michael. "He's a scout."

"You think he's here to watch Elijah?" asked Dylan.

"He ain't here to look at my fat ass," said Michael. "Let's make our boy look good out there."

They opened the gate and walked, single file, to the center of the court. Elijah gathered his teammates around him and put his hand in the middle; the others did the same. "We don't need fancy speeches, do we?"

"No," said Dylan.

"Uh-uh," said Michael.

"Because we've been playing on these courts since we were little. This is our home."

His teammates nodded.

"So let's get out there and show them how we treat people who try to take our home," said Elijah.

The referee, a middle-aged guy with a gray brush cut, gave the opening instructions. "Bags and gear against the fence, boys. You got three minutes to warm up." They dropped their bags and sat down to watch their opponents.

"You don't want to warm up?" the ref added.

Elijah shook his head. "We're ready, sir. Just tell us when it's time to start."

The ref shrugged and called for the Shooters' captain, who couldn't have been more than five-foot-seven on a good day. He looked fit, though, and had a springy walk that suggested his legs might have a couple of surprising moves in them. His teammates were taller but not by much.

"Nice uniforms," said the Shooters' captain. "How much those cost?"

"I don't know yet," said Elijah. "Haven't gotten the bill."

"Okay," said the ref. "Game's ten minutes long with twenty-one-point sudden death. Field goals are one point each. Anything beyond the white arc is two points. Observe the take-back line on any conversion, and remember, all free throws are dead balls. No questions? Good."

32

ELIJAH LINED UP defensively with his teammates. He checked the ball back to the Shooters' captain and then waited for him to pass it back into play. It was not a good start. The little man snuck a quick bounce pass under Elijah's arm. His teammate shook Michael loose, and as soon as he caught the pass, he hurled it at the backboard. It wasn't even close! The ball floated like a big orange moon until the third guy, the captain again—all five-foot-seven of him—leapt over Dylan's head and tipped it through the iron.

Elijah shook his head in disbelief. "Nice shot."

"Thanks, man," said the captain.

Dylan carried the ball to the line looking more than a little sheepish. "Did you see that? Little dude can jump!"

"I saw it." Elijah smiled and stuck out his hand for a slap. "Now how about we show that scout over there how fast you are?"

"Okay by me. I can feel my ADD kicking in; I haven't taken my meds in three days. Saving up my energy."

As the game developed, both teams traded points, neither yielding an advantage. At the twenty-minute mark, Elijah clamped a hand on Michael's shoulder. "We need a turnover, bro. You ready to do your thing?"

Michael nodded, understanding. "I've been waiting for you to call it."

At the sound of the ref's whistle, Elijah dropped deep, guarding his man loosely, giving up way too much real estate north of the foul line. But he knew Michael was behind him, crouched low, just waiting for the shooter to plant his feet. And when he did, Elijah peeled to the side; Michael pushed off on his thick, powerful legs. He rose up high for a man of his breadth and swatted the ball with one oven-mitt of a hand, spinning it off his fingertips. Two players launched into the air for the rebound, both acutely aware that the fate of the game might be at stake.

If there had been any question as to who would return to earth with the ball, Elijah answered it with an exclamation point, sharp elbows scissoring the air to protect his newly acquired possession. His Kobe 10s touched down on the pavement for a microsecond and then bounded away toward the take-back line.

Elijah paced the backcourt with the ball, looking for an opening. Any opening. But the opposing team's captain was practically glued to him, poking and whipping his arms in a desperate attempt to strip the ball. Elijah dished it to Dylan, who drew the captain's attention and then hooked it right back into Elijah's hands. Elijah spun and pivoted, blowing by the second guard. But as he approached the last man back, Elijah appeared to step—no, climb through the air—over him, feeling every bit like a force of destiny bent on rolling the leather off his outstretched fingers and into the ring of steel.

Elijah had no clue that he'd caught the attention of the scout, who had just burned his lips on a cup of scalding coffee. "Jesus," he said to a couple of guys standing next to him. "Did you see that?"

Even if Elijah had known, he wouldn't have cared, because at that moment, he had transcended himself. Gone were any thoughts of the tournament, or even his teammates. Airborne, arms stretched high and wide, he had entered that elusive place of basketball perfection where time flows in a circle instead of beating like a geared clock or a fallible heart. He had become movement. Purpose. Grace.

But the other team wasn't ready to give in. They bore down in the final minutes and worked the inside with quick passes and a clever reverse layup; it rolled the lip of the rim dangerously, and popped out.

Twenty-five seconds left on the clock.

Michael snagged the rebound and heaved it to Elijah, who backpedaled toward the line. As soon as he toed the paint, he loosed a high floater to Michael, who pulled it down safely and handed it off to a sprinting Dylan.

Ten seconds.

Dylan dipped one shoulder and then the other but made no move. His guard crouched, low and nervous, waiting. No one on either team knew what the hell he was doing; he was too far back for a shot, and yet he made no move toward the goal.

Three seconds.

Dylan stopped dribbling and straightened his body. The rest of the players could only watch, helpless, as his feet lifted gently off the pavement for a perfect jumper. It was too risky a shot, at least eight feet behind the two-point line. But the ball dropped through the net with barely a ripple. Elijah's Army had won their first game.

33

THE SECOND GAME, which was technically a quarterfinal, was over almost as soon as it had begun. Every player on the Pete's Irish Pub team—clad in vintage Boston Celtics uniforms—was a sharpshooter, which should have spelled doom for Elijah's Army. Fortunately, they were also well into their thirties and forties and possessed the soft, paunchy middles and bandy legs to prove it.

Two minutes after the initial whistle, Elijah's Army was up, seven to two. Five minutes later, they ended the game by scoring twenty-one points.

"We're doing it," said Dylan.

"Hell, yes," said Michael.

But there was little time to celebrate as the boys were ushered straight into their next game. This time the players on the opposing team were enormous, all well over six feet, with broad, muscular shoulders. Each one was covered in tattoos: tribal symbols, snakes, and a couple of naked women. One guy, the forward, had a scaled serpent wrapping itself around a massive shoulder and arm. The tattoos contrasted vividly against white jerseys with the team name spelled out in dripping crimson: Killer Ink.

"Whoa," said Dylan. "Remember that dude?"

Elijah looked up to see Neck Tattoo, the bruiser they'd seen playing weeks before. He wore mirrored sunglasses and a Raiders cap turned backward.

"I'm not guarding him," said Dylan. "No way."

"Come on," said Elijah. "Nobody in this tournament can touch your game. You can believe it or not, but either way it's true."

"That dude scares me," said Dylan. "He's freaking intimidating."

The captain of the other team—the one with the serpent—didn't shake Elijah's hand or wish them a good game. Instead, he sucked his teeth and then spat, as though the sight of Elijah gave him a bad taste that needed to be gotten rid of.

"I know about you," he said.

Elijah frowned but said nothing.

"I ain't afraid of Money, and I sure as hell ain't afraid of you."

"Good for you," said Elijah. "Nice neck tattoo, by the way. It makes you look tough."

Throughout the first half of the game, Elijah's Army struggled to break through the opposing team's defense. Every time they tried, Killer Ink drove them back relentlessly, forcing them to take jumpers and outside shots. But Elijah could see the frustration in Neck Tattoo's eyes; he hadn't expected real competition from a bunch of high school kids.

Late in the second half, Elijah decided to try something crazy. Instead of checking the ball to Neck Tattoo, he rolled it ever so gently. Neck Tattoo watched it, incredulous, and then responded by firing it back at Elijah's head. Elijah hit the pavement to avoid being decapitated as the ball sailed out of bounds and into the fence. A high blast of the referee's whistle brought everyone to attention. The small, paunchy man in the black-and-white-striped shirt approached.

"You," he said to Neck Tattoo. "Come here."

While the ref gave his lecture, Elijah used the time to huddle with his team. "Okay, listen up. On offense, I'll find a way through. On defense, force Neck Tattoo to his left. He'll want to push back around to his right, but don't let him. Use your body, and plant your feet if you have to. One free throw is going to win this game."

"Okay," said Michael. "Maybe we'll get lucky and he'll twist his ankle stepping on Dylan's face."

"Very funny." Dylan offered a morose grin.

After another check-in that was only slightly less murderous, Elijah dished it to Dylan, who was quickly wrapped up and passed it back. Just as quickly, Neck Tattoo jumped into Elijah's face, bumping him with his chest, half an inch shy of a foul. Elijah allowed himself to be bullied back to the line, where he dribbled, high and loose, waiting.

Dylan read the setup and streaked from the backcourt as Elijah shot a bounce pass between the big man's legs. Dylan took the pass on the run and drew a foul as he put up what should have been an easy layup. But the blow to the back of his neck sent him sprawling, and the ball rolled twice around the rim before it dropped through. The crowd went nuts.

34

IT TOOK DYLAN a full minute to pick the bits of gravel from his knees and elbows. But he toed the foul line with a big smile, waving and blowing kisses to his new and adoring fans.

Elijah patted him on the back. "You got this."

"I know." Dylan bounced the ball once and then buried his free throw. The final score at the ten-minute mark: sixteen to fourteen.

Elijah leaned back against the fence as Dylan and Michael were practically swallowed up by dozens waiting to shake hands and congratulate them. One man stepped from the crowd and waved to Elijah. He wore a white polo shirt with an orange Syracuse cap.

"Elijah," he said. "I'm Sam Lehigh, from Syracuse University."

"Hi." Elijah didn't believe it, but he shook the man's hand anyway. It had to be a joke.

"Your coach, Bernie Walters, has been talking a lot about you." Sam pointed to a nearby bench. "Can we sit for a minute?"

"Yes," said Elijah. "I mean, yes, sir."

✳ ✳ ✳

THE WHOLE WAY HOME, Elijah studied Sam Lehigh's business card. He turned it over and over, trying to find the flaw that would reveal it as a fake. But it was real enough. Across the front, orange-and-blue lettering said: *Sam Lehigh, Recruiting, Syracuse University, Carmelo K. Anthony Center, Syracuse NY 13244.* And on the back, a personal cell number.

"We'll talk more after your game tomorrow," Sam had said. "But call that number in the meantime if you or your mother have any questions I can answer."

Elijah was nearly delirious with excitement when he burst through the front door. Syracuse University. His mother wouldn't believe it. But he'd show her the business card, and she'd see. What she really wouldn't believe was the fantasy he'd built up around his father coming to watch him play in the finals. A part of him knew it was childish, but hadn't his mother said dreams were important? Well, this was his dream, and he was ready to make it come true.

HIS MOTHER SAT rigid at the kitchen table, hands folded primly on top of each other. She did not get up or look at him.

"What's wrong?" Elijah dropped into a chair.

But she didn't say anything. Instead, she shook her head from side to side.

"What's the matter?" he said. "We won all three of our games today! That means we're in the finals tomorrow."

"You are not playing in any game tomorrow."

"What are you talking about?" he said. "We won, Mom."

"Oh, Elijah. How could you?"

He studied her face, trying to piece together what was wrong, what he'd done to disappoint her so much.

"I went with Dylan's and Michael's mother to watch you play," she began. "We couldn't get close enough because there were so many people, but they had a big TV set up by one of those news vans."

His mind raced to find a connection—Dylan's mother, one of the ESPN vans. Nothing. There was no connection.

"We got to see you and your friends on TV, playing. I was so proud, of course."

She pulled a tissue from one of her pockets and dabbed at the corner of her eye. "But then someone else who was watching—a boy no older than you—said to his friend, 'Do you see that little patch on their jerseys? Do you know what it means? What it stands for?'"

And then he got it, the full weight of her disappointment. "Mom, let me explain."

But she held up a hand. "What's to explain? I'm not a fool, Elijah."

He hung his head.

"How could you do this? We worked so hard to make a good life for ourselves. Just the two of us. Nobody helped. I know it hasn't been easy. You don't have the same expensive shoes and clothes as Michael and the other kids at school. But I think we've done just fine."

"I don't care about those things, Mom."

She reached across the table and pulled at the little round patch. "Then why this? I don't understand."

"Because I didn't want you to get hurt."

"How would I get hurt? This has nothing to do with me. Don't you dare put this on me."

He took the picture from his wallet and handed it to her.

"Explain what this is supposed to mean?" she said, but her fingers trembled.

And when she'd heard enough, she pulled a pair of scissors from the telephone drawer and cut the picture into pieces. Then threw the pieces into the trash.

"Elijah, don't you understand? They've already hurt me. By getting to you, they've won."

Elijah thought for a moment before speaking. How could he explain the truth without hurting his mother's feelings? That maybe he couldn't do everything on his own and he needed a father, a role model, to help him learn how to be a man.

"I don't know what to do, Mom. I don't know how to fix this. If I resist, people might hurt you. And I can't let that happen. But if I go along with it . . . well, you know."

She looked away. "I understand, Son, but you're not playing tomorrow. That's how you deal with this situation."

"Mom."

"I will not have you wearing that awful patch. Blood Street Nation."

"It will be worse if I don't play."

"How could it be worse?"

He pictured his father in the crowd, watching, waiting. And then the announcer telling everyone that the game was canceled. But his mother didn't know about any of that; she was talking about the gang. "You don't know these people."

"That's right. I'm proud that I don't know them. And I don't want you to know them, either. Which means you can stay home, or play as yourselves."

"What do you mean?"

"Wear what you used to wear, T-shirts and old sneakers. You'll be on television again, right?"

"Yes," said Elijah. "The finals are always televised."

"Then go and play on television as yourselves. I want the world to see that my son is not in a gang. I want the world to know you're a good boy and not a criminal."

"Mom."

"It's that or not playing at all. Your choice." And then, "I'd move us out of here tomorrow if I had enough money. So that's the best I can think of."

Elijah looked at his hands; his fingers were long, perfectly designed for palming a basketball. His legs were lean and powerful, suited for jumping. He'd felt himself getting better with each game, had developed an awareness that allowed him to see plays developing before anyone else could perceive them. He was meant to play ball. What would he do without it? How would he meet his father? And then there was Sam Lehigh's business card. He'd come so close.

"What's that?" asked his mother when she saw the card.

"Nothing." Elijah slid the card along his palm and went to his room.

35

WITHIN AN HOUR, Elijah's mother had organized a full team meeting in their living room. Mothers and sons occupied the couch and the kitchen chairs. Dylan and Michael tried to goof and keep it light, but they knew that something big was up. Elijah was the first to speak. He tried to be strong and look his friends in the eye, but inside he felt like he'd let everyone down. If only he'd said no that day at school, when Michael had shown them the shoes. He could have. Sure, his friends would have been upset, but they'd have gotten over it. And they wouldn't be in this mess.

Elijah cleared his throat. "I've been talking to my mother and doing some thinking. If I'm still the captain of our team, I want us to play tomorrow in our own clothes. No BSN jerseys. No Kobe 10s. Instead, we'll be ourselves—three best friends from the neighborhood who can play ball better than anyone else out there."

Dylan wrinkled his brow, thinking, trying to understand.

Michael started to open his mouth to object, but his mother slapped him hard across the back of his head.

"I did not raise a fool, Michael Allen Henderson. I've looked the other way too many times over the years. No more. You hear me?"

"Mom," said Michael. "You don't understand. There's gonna be consequences."

"Boy, don't even try to tell me I don't understand. You want to talk about consequences? I'll give you consequences you don't even know about." She braced one hand on her hip, the other extended toward her son. "Hand over that jersey."

Michael tightened his jaw but said nothing.

"Now," said his mother.

With great reluctance, Michael handed over the plastic bag that contained his clothes. Dylan did the same without any argument.

Later, when some of the tension had drained, Elijah's mother poured glasses of wine for the women. They talked in the kitchen about what else they could do to keep their boys safe. Talk to the police. And Pastor Fredericks. Check in with each other every night, to make sure they were accounted for and safe. The boys listened for a few minutes and then retreated to the front steps.

Michael was the first to speak. "This ain't okay. I'm just saying."

"We'll deal with it," said Elijah. "Clothes don't make us a team."

"Sure," said Dylan, "but they were nice. Are we really going back to our old kicks?"

"Unless you want to face all those women in there," said Elijah.

"I definitely do not," said Dylan.

Michael sat, brooding. "You two don't understand; it ain't about the clothes. It's what they represent. You just don't do this to people like Money and Blood Street. It ain't okay. There's consequences."

"Right," said Elijah, unable to swallow his anger any longer. "Which means you were stringing us along when you said it was just ball. Nothing to do with the gang. That's what you said."

"It is just ball, but the man put out a lot for them shoes and jerseys. How are we going to say we ain't wearing them anymore? How's that going to look? Like disrespect. Like a great big 'Screw you.'"

"We'll pay him back," said Elijah. "That way he won't be out anything."

"Whoa," said Dylan. "Hang on a second. You know I'm broke."

"We're one game away from three thousand dollars," said Elijah. "We win the tournament and each put in an equal share to pay back the money."

Michael waved the idea away with his hand. "I told you, it ain't about the clothes, and it ain't about the money."

"What's it about, then?" asked Dylan.

"Respect and loyalty, man. We said we'd play for Money and wear his kicks. Now we're saying no. He's not gonna let that slide."

They sat silently, side by side on the top step. Michael rubbed his eyes with the heels of his hands. Tilting his head back to look at the dark sky, he said, "You two gonna be all right, probably. But I'm gonna have to explain this shit to Money. And you know what he's gonna say?"

"What?" asked Dylan.

"He's gonna say, 'You screwed up, dawg. I was counting on you, and you failed. Now you got to fix it.'"

"Fix it how?" asked Dylan.

"Man, I don't know. If I knew that, I'd just do it now and make things right."

"Then go back in there." Dylan gestured in the direction of the front door. "Explain it and change their minds. I'll do whatever you two think is best. I love my moms, but she doesn't know how it really is. Man, she still thinks my brother, Marvin, is innocent. I love my brother, but he ain't her sweet little boy no more."

"Damn," said Michael, standing up. "I'm more afraid of my mom than I am of Blood Street. I'll see you two tomorrow."

"Hey," called Elijah. "You're still with us, right? We're still a team?"

"Yeah," said Michael. "We're a team. I just gotta go home and think."

36

IT WAS AFTER nine by the time Elijah's mother said goodbye to her guests. She poured herself a second glass of wine and sat down across from Elijah. Her face was drawn with fatigue. She looked like she'd aged several years in one night.

"Don't worry," he said. "We'll be okay."

"I don't know if I made the right decision. Michael's mother agrees about the jerseys, but she says gangs retaliate. What if that happens, Elijah?"

"It'll be fine." But he didn't believe it. There was the picture of his mother. And Money's comments. *From now on Blood Street Nation's your family.*

"I want to believe that so much, Son. I really do." She held her glass to her lips but then set it down and pushed it away. "Can you call Coach Walters? He understands these things. He'll know just what to do."

"Can't," said Elijah. "He's gone until school starts back up, remember?"

"How about Pastor Fredericks? He works with all kinds of young people. Maybe he can help."

"No offense, Mom, but that's a terrible idea. He's a nice guy, but this is way out of his league."

"Well, there's got to be someone," she said.

ELIJAH LEFT HIS mother in the kitchen and walked with his head down toward the Battlegrounds. She didn't want to let him out of her sight, but he said he was going to meet Michael and Dylan for a final strategy session. A lie, of course, but he needed to think. If he and his friends were going to openly defy Money and Blood Street Nation, he had to have a plan.

At the courts, all the garbage cans had been emptied, and the fences were covered with signs and banners announcing the championship game. Across the street, the neon sign in the window of Antonio's Pizzeria blazed, but he didn't feel like eating; instead, he walked on until he found himself at Banks's house. He climbed the front steps and knocked on the door.

"Hi," said Kerri. "Isn't it a little late to start working?"

"I'm not working."

"That's right. You've got a baseball tournament or something."

"Basketball, but that was in the morning."

Kerri grinned. "I know it's basketball. Do you want to come in?"

"I was hoping I could talk to your father," said Elijah.

"You mean you don't want to talk to me?" Kerri made a sad face.

"I do. I mean, I would, but . . ."

"I'm just messing with you. He's downstairs. Come on in." Kerri led him through the living room and kitchen and down a steep, narrow staircase.

Machine noise echoed off the concrete walls of a basement woodshop with Peg-Board-lined walls, a lumber rack, a workbench, and several contractor-grade power tools. In the center of the workshop Banks stood over a table saw, trying to force a cut through a board that wasn't cooperating. Acrid, black smoke filled the air, along with a terrible whining noise.

"Goddammit." Banks jumped back as his board jammed and then shot backward, barely missing his hip.

Kerri waved to get her father's attention. He flipped a switch on the front panel and stepped away from the protesting machine. "What? I'm working."

Kerri jerked her thumb in Elijah's direction, then turned on her heel and went back up the stairs.

Elijah hunched to avoid hitting his head on the roof joists, which just cleared the bristles of Banks's crew cut. "I'm sorry to bother you."

"It's fine. I'm probably going to cut off a finger anyway."

"I didn't know you had a woodshop."

"It came with the house. I thought I'd try a project, but . . ." Banks brushed sawdust from his forehead. "What's up—did I forget to pay you?"

"No." Elijah's eyes fell away from Banks and onto the table saw. The teeth of the blade were scorched and dull, a dangerous combination that his shop teacher, Mr. Lemke, would never have tolerated.

"What is it, then?"

"I've got a problem."

"What, you need more money? I'm not giving you an advance. You've done a good job so far, but you still have to work for—"

"I don't need money, but if you don't want to hear me out, that's fine. I mean, we don't really know each other, and I get it. You don't even like me."

Banks brushed sawdust off his arms. "Listen, I don't like anybody, but that's got nothing to do with you. Come on up to the kitchen and tell me what's on your mind."

37

BANKS LISTENED INTENTLY as Elijah explained about Money and the basketball tournament. He did not interrupt, nor did he have questions.

"It's your basic catch-22," he said at the end of the story.

Elijah nodded, uncertain if the phrase meant "damned if you do . . ." or if it was a reference to the book title, which he thought had something to do with war.

"And you want me to tell you how to get out of it? You can't get out of a catch-22. That's exactly *why* it's a catch-22."

"But there's got to be something I can do." Elijah thought he heard footsteps in the next room, possibly from Kerri listening in on their conversation.

"Sure. There's always something you can do, but don't expect a clean getaway."

"What should I expect?"

"Hypothetically?"

"Yes," said Elijah.

"To incur some damage. But if you intervene the right way, you should have some control over which pieces fall and where. When it all blows up, that is."

"I don't get it," said Elijah. "I've got two choices: I can join the gang or go against it. Whichever one I pick, I lose control once the choice is made."

"That's good logical thinking," said Banks. "But it's dead wrong. Let's say you want to knock down a building. How would you do it?"

"I don't know. I'd use a wrecking ball or a backhoe shovel, I guess."

"No good. Assuming you have one of those—which you don't—it's way too big. Too loud. Too obvious." Banks grabbed a piece of paper and a pencil and quickly sketched a small, square structure with a peaked roof. "Okay, here's the building, and say you want to knock it down quietly, secretly, so that when it falls, no one will even suspect that you did it."

Elijah couldn't see how any of this related. "I'm dealing with a gang. Why would I want to knock a building down?"

"Because in this case the building represents something more complicated and insidious, like a gang. They both have a structure that can be bolstered or weakened."

"Okay," said Elijah. "I'm with you."

"So the real question is whether you're content putting a little hole in the roof or you'd rather bring the entire structure down on itself."

"The entire structure. Definitely."

"Right. Now think. How would you do it? Where's the weak point, and how much do you need to push on it?"

"I don't know." Elijah studied the picture. He realized that at some point Banks had undergone a complete personality transformation. He was actually personable. Animated. Using complete sentences. "I could go inside and pull—"

"You can't," said Banks. "Because the roof would fall right on top of you. Here's the rules." Beneath the drawing, he wrote the following in his perfect, machinelike hand:

You must cause the building to implode or collapse on itself.
The demolition will cause no physical harm to you.
The demolition will not be attributed to you.

Elijah turned the paper, examining it from different angles.

"Come on," said Banks. "We'll do this live. But no questions. I want you thinking for yourself; ask one more question, and we're done. Understand?"

"Yes."

"Good."

38

BANKS HUSTLED OUT the back door and through the yard, which was still cluttered with piles of brush and concrete chunks. He ducked inside the toolshed and grabbed a coil of black rope. "This is nine-and-a-half-millimeter static line. Strong stuff. See if you can use it to knock the shed down without breaking any of the three rules."

"You want me to destroy your shed," said Elijah.

"It's crap anyway. I'll bring the Jeep over; you'll need the light."

It took Elijah fifteen minutes to carry the shovels, rakes, and mattocks from the shed to the small single-car garage. Banks positioned the Jeep so that the headlights illuminated a swath of backyard surrounding the shed. Clouds of mosquitoes formed around the halogens, providing a rich feeding ground for a dozen or so bats that cut back and forth through the light.

Banks thumped Elijah on the back. "Take your time and think it through. I'll be downstairs. Come get me when you're done."

Elijah studied the inside of the shed. He considered each stud, rafter, and cinder block for its structural importance, trying to find the weak point. The foundation and walls looked solid, but the corner studs were all loose. Happy with this discovery, he used a power drill to bore holes at the tops and bottoms of the studs; through these, he ran loops of rope that he cut and tied off. Lastly, he ran the black static line through the loops such that the line would exert equal pressure on each of them. He was so focused on his work that he failed to notice Kerri standing in the doorway, talking to him.

"I think you're doing it wrong," she said.

"What?"

"I heard you two talking about implosion. If you want this thing to fall in on itself, I'd pull just from the bottom loops. And you have to concentrate the force from the center; otherwise you'll just pull it over to one side, which won't be as clean as a true collapse."

Elijah wiped the sweat from his face with his shirt. "How do you know?"

"I took physics," she said. "And I did two weeks with Habitat for Humanity, so I know how a building goes up. Just reverse the process to take it down, right?"

Elijah sat back and considered; he saw that she was right. From the top would work better, and he'd need to run the static line through another loop in the center. "You're very strange. Do you know that?"

Kerri nodded. "So are you. My father works you like a dog, and you keep coming back. Why? There must be easier ways to make money."

"I don't know," said Elijah. "I don't like to quit."

He tested his work and made adjustments until the rope pulled equally on the corner studs. "What's your father making down there anyway?"

"He's *trying* to make a display case for his medals, but it's not going so well, if you ask me."

"I didn't think accountants got medals."

"They don't, and he's not an accountant; that's just what he tells people when he doesn't want to explain. But listen, I have a confession. Would you like to hear it?"

"Yes!" Elijah answered a little too enthusiastically.

"Oh, get over yourself," said Kerri. "Not that kind of confession."

"Right." Elijah tried to play it cool, though he suspected it was too late for that.

"I listened to your whole conversation. Not just the part about tearing down the building."

"You were eavesdropping," said Elijah.

"So? I'm bored out of my mind here. Anyway, about your gang problem—I think I know how to fix it. Which is another way of saying that I've got a plan."

Elijah looked in the direction of the house; Banks was opening the back door, coming out to check on him. "A plan."

"Yes. A simple, elegant one to destroy the gang and solve your problem." Kerri pressed a slip of paper into his palm. "Call me after your silly basketball tournament and I'll explain it to you. It's not a date, though."

"Of course it wouldn't be a date," said Elijah. "Why would I think that?"

"Good," said Kerri. "I'm glad you understand. By the way, I don't really think your tournament is silly."

AFTER BANKS SHOOED his daughter back to a safe distance, he inspected Elijah's work, tugging on each and every line and knot. "Not bad. Your rope work is as ugly as hell, but it'll hold."

"Is there a rule against using this winch?" Elijah tapped the spool of steel cable on the Jeep's front bumper.

"Have at it," said Banks. "You ever used one before?"

"No, but I'll figure it out." Elijah found the release lever and pulled out ten feet of cable. Next, he secured the black rope to the safety hook on the end of the cable. "Ready?"

Banks and Kerri stood off to the side, waiting.

Elijah pushed a red button on the winch's housing; a low electric whine issued as the cable snaked smoothly around the barrel and lifted the black rope off the ground. As it drew taut, the building creaked once and shuddered. Elijah backed away.

39

THE BOYS DRESSED in plain gray sweats and marched solemnly to the Battlegrounds. They didn't speak or pass the ball around. Each was absorbed in his thoughts, but Elijah knew his friends well enough to guess what was running through their minds. Dylan was probably mixed between excitement for the game and sorrow over the loss of his new shoes. Michael was undoubtedly worried about Money. As for Elijah, he knew he should have been thinking about the exact moment when he would recognize his father's face in the crowd. But instead, he replayed in his mind the destruction of Banks's shed . . . the way the rope had drawn as taut as a wire, pulling the walls down with a muffled thump. And how neatly the roof had fallen on top of the whole mess. Much more gently and quietly than he would have expected.

And the best part was what Banks had said: "Nicely done, boy. Clean and effective." It wasn't much, but he knew compliments were rare from Banks. And he *had* done a good job. He'd followed the rules and taken down the shed cleanly and effectively. He had a right to be proud. There was something else, too—the little slip of paper that contained Kerri's phone number. *It's not a date,* she'd said. Which meant that she'd at least thought about the possibility of a date with him.

Nearing the Battlegrounds, Elijah's limbs began to tingle. It was a familiar feeling, a jagged current of energy he knew would explode on the court in a storm of layups, jumpers, and drives. He wiggled his toe through the hole in his shoe, glad to be free of his nicer but tainted kicks.

At the edge of the parking lot, which was packed to overflowing with cars, SUVs, and several news vans, Dylan stopped and turned to face them. "I can't take any more of this doom-and-gloom crap. I mean, didn't we train all year just to get here? So how come we're acting like someone's dog got run over? None of us has a dog."

"Because," said Elijah, remembering. "We're about to dis Blood Street Nation in front of hundreds of people. We're going to have to pay for that."

"There ain't no *we*." Michael scowled. "I'm the one that's gonna have to pay. I'm the one putting himself on the line."

Dylan's face grew red. "That's crap, Michael. Ain't we standing here with you? Ain't we by your side? We always got your back."

"Yeah, you're here," said Michael. "But you're here to play some ball. That's different."

"No, it ain't," said Dylan. "It's all the same for me. On the court or off. I love you guys. We're brothers, and it's always gonna be like that."

Elijah touched Dylan on the shoulder. "Well said, brother." He looked off in the distance at court number one, which was lined on both sides with hundreds of people. He wondered if Sam Lehigh was among them, and if he was waiting to see him play again. It was a selfish thought, but he wished they could save this argument for later. Because what he really wanted to do more than anything was play. Why couldn't they forget about Money and Blood Street Nation and play ball?

"Grow up, Dylan," said Michael. "What do you think's gonna happen to us? We ain't gonna stick together, and you know it."

"That ain't true," said Dylan.

"It is," said Michael. "Elijah's gonna go off to college and be with smart people. Better people than us. You wait and see. And we gonna be watching him on TV and saying, 'That's our boy Elijah Thomas!' Only he ain't gonna be our boy anymore 'cause he'll be gone."

"That doesn't mean we won't still—"

"Man, that's *exactly* what it means. Don't you get it? He's gonna go *be somebody*. Didn't you see him talking to that scout? Don't you know what that means?"

"Yeah. So?"

"So he's set, and you and me . . . well, we gonna be right here fighting thugs like Bull and Neck Tattoo for whatever scraps is left."

Dylan shook his head and looked down at his worn-out sneaks. "I don't know about you, but I'm gonna be somebody, too. You wait and see."

"You keep believing that, Dylan," said Michael, stalking away toward the courts.

"Screw you!" Dylan's eyes brimmed with tears. "Man, who do you think sticks up for you when people say stuff behind your back, like about how you're all arrogant and only care about yourself? I do. Me. I tell them they're wrong about you. I tell them, 'He's a good guy; you just don't know him. Michael's got a big heart; he just doesn't like to show it.'"

"Maybe they're right," said Michael. "Maybe I'm not a good guy."

"Come on, man." Elijah caught up and placed his hand on Michael's shoulder.

Michael shrugged off his hand. "You don't want to hear it, Elijah, but it's true. I was so jealous you had your future all lined up. I started thinking, 'He's gonna get it all, and what do you got, Michael? Nothing.'" He looked away, like he was talking to someone else. "So I went and talked to Money and started hustling, trying to make a name for myself."

"Hustling. What's that mean? How you been hustling?" asked Dylan.

"Started out running errands and stuff. But then it was things you wouldn't even believe. Bad things. It's like you cross this one line," said Michael. "And it's a big deal and you're afraid to cross it. But you do it again and it ain't as scary; it's easier. And then one day you look at yourself in the mirror and you're, like, a different person."

Elijah studied his hands; he didn't trust himself to look at his friend.

"So when Money wanted to sponsor a player—someone good enough to get a shot at a Big Ten school—I was like, 'You got to see my boy Elijah.'"

"The shoes and jerseys were your idea," said Elijah.

"That's right." Michael straightened, wiping at his eyes with the heels of his hands. "It wasn't all selfish, though. You were running around out there with your toes busting through your sneaks, and I thought you deserved better. I thought you deserved your chance. Then Money saw you play and wanted to know if I could make it happen. I jumped at the opportunity and said, 'Hell, yeah, I can.'"

"And you did," said Elijah.

"Almost." Michael lifted up his sweatshirt to show their plain white T-shirts. "Now we're back to ourselves, and Money's gonna put a cap in me. I probably deserve it." He flashed a quick smile and turned to walk away, toward the crowd that was gathering around the center court, where they were scheduled to play. "Come on. We got a game to win."

40

"ELIJAH'S ARMY?" said the volunteer at the check-in table.

"We're changing our name," said Elijah.

"What?" The volunteer scanned the boys' faces to make sure he'd heard correctly.

"We're not Elijah's Army no more," said Michael.

"Well, who are you, then?" said the volunteer.

Elijah looked at the dry-erase board. Since Elijah's Army was listed in the sixteenth slot, he said, "We're Team 16."

The volunteer stared at him, unblinking. Finally, he shrugged and said, "Okay, fine. Team 16 it is. I need to see your wristbands."

Dylan and Michael stepped forward and pulled up the sleeves of their sweatshirts.

"And you?" said the volunteer.

Elijah hesitated, thinking about what Michael had said. *Before Money puts a cap in me.* Was that really a possibility? Then he remembered Ray Shiver. Why wouldn't it be possible?

"Come on, man," said Michael. "What's done is done. Let's just play ball, and I'll deal with Money later." He put his hand on his friend's back and shoved him gently toward the table.

Elijah struggled to get the thick, heavy words out of his mouth. "Are we friends? You and me and Dylan."

Michael sighed but said nothing.

Elijah fought the surge of emotions that threatened to overwhelm him. "Michael, look at me, man. Are we friends?"

"Yeah." Michael sniffed and wiped at his nose. "But that don't mean—"

Elijah held up his hand. "If that's still true, then we've got your back. Period."

Michael scuffed the toe of one of his sneakers. When he looked up, his eyes were red and filled with tears. "So what's that mean? You don't hate me for setting you up? Because that's what I did, man. I set you up."

"It means that after we win this game, we're going to deal with Money together. All three of us."

THE TOURNAMENT COORDINATOR gave a quick blast of an air horn to get everyone's attention. "And now the moment you've all been waiting for! Competing for the grand prize of three thousand dollars and the 2014 Hoops title, I am proud to present two of the most exciting street ball teams you'll ever see."

Cheers and whistles rose up through the crowd and engulfed the speaker in a wave of sound. "First, with an average player age of twenty-four, I present the returning Hoops champions, Blunt Force Trauma!"

The team made their way out to the first court in silver metallic tracksuits, with their names and numbers on the back—Basher, number one; Skillz, number seven; and Big Al, number ninety-nine. Basher couldn't have weighed a pound under two-sixty, and yet he moved with the ease and athleticism of a much smaller player, dribbling and cutting his way to a clean reverse layup. Skillz had the perfect build for a street baller: six-foot two, and strong and lean. For a warm-up, he stopped at the nineteen-foot arc and dropped four consecutive two-pointers before tossing the ball to Big Al, their aptly named forward. Big Al stood six-foot-eight and could slam it from the foul line with enough authority to make many teams give up on the spot.

"Last but not least," said the announcer. "Formerly known as Elijah's Army, with an average player age of seventeen, Team 16!"

The boys stood at the gate, listening to scattered applause from a bewildered crowd. The boys wore old, dirty sneakers that had lost their jump long ago—from walking all over town, not to mention countless Battleground pickup games. And in place of their hundred-dollar custom jerseys, they each wore a white Hanes. On the front of each T-shirt, the boys had hastily written "Team 16" with a black Sharpie. Elijah wondered if people perceived them as nervous boys dressed in half-assed clothes or as young men taking a stand. And what of Sam Lehigh? How would he see them? Or their mothers, who watched silently and nervously from the front row of the crowd.

The announcer continued, "Folks, keep your eyes on these three exciting young players, all of them upcoming seniors on the varsity team at Montgomery High School, the pride and joy of Baltimore's own Coach Bernie Walters. Give it up for Team 16!"

The boys walked to center court, where they stood shoulder to shoulder. They looked at the crowd gathered beyond the fence, at least a hundred persons deep. Elijah knew he should look for Sam, the Syracuse scout, but his eyes were busy scanning every tallish African American male in his late thirties. A few were possibilities, but the skin tone or facial structure was off.

Dylan nudged Elijah and pointed at Elijah's mother who stood at the front of the crowd next to the scout. "They're here for you."

"Let's go," said the referee.

"We're ready, sir," said Elijah. Dylan and Michael stood on either side of him, relaxed, ready.

BUT THEY WEREN'T READY. For one, Dylan and Michael were badly mismatched, neither of them able to outmaneuver or out-muscle their opponents. And Elijah, who was usually the epitome of grace under pressure, was so distracted that an easy pass bounced right off his head.

"What's wrong with you, man?" said Michael after they lost their first possession on a rare brick that bounced off the top of the backboard.

But to answer his question all Michael needed to do was follow Elijah's gaze to behind the far goalpost, where Money glared at them, vengeful, seething.

"Oh, damn," said Michael as the hooded figure raised his hand in the shape of a gun. He lowered his thumb, the universal gesture to symbolize pulling a trigger.

41

THE NEXT TWELVE minutes were a study in confusion. The Blunt Force players dominated every aspect of the game, while Team 16 looked like they'd just woken up.

In the fourth minute, Elijah nailed a pair of two-pointers and a jaw-dropping reverse dunk; but over- or underthrown passes immediately followed, along with quick conversions by Big Al. On defense, Team 16 collapsed on drives and conceded too much space on the outside for easy jumpers. At the twelve-minute mark, the score was thirteen to ten in favor of Blunt Force Trauma.

"Time-out!" said Elijah.

"I got nothing left," huffed Michael, looking down at his feet. "They're schooling me out there."

"Yeah," said Dylan, shaking his head. "How come I feel slow?"

Elijah scanned the fence line, looking for Money; thankfully, he was gone. He slapped his teammates lightly. "Let's cut the crap out there, okay? We're better than this."

"What do you want us to do? They're too strong." Michael wiped sweat off his face and shook it from his hands.

"I want you to stop acting scared and play our game," said Elijah.

"What's our game again?" asked Dylan.

Elijah knew he was supposed to say something to motivate his teammates. But all he could think about was yesterday morning, and how they'd still been friends. He remembered walking down the middle of the street, playing Switch, their stupid passing game that really wasn't stupid at all, now that he thought about it. It was the embodiment of their style, because it was based on how well they knew each other—to the point where they could anticipate each other's movements so far in advance. And that was exactly what was missing.

"Our game is that we've been playing ball together our whole lives. Isn't this our home?"

"Yeah," said Michael and Dylan together. "This is our home."

"Then let's play like it. Let's relax and switch it up a little bit." He grinned at his friends until they understood.

"You want us to play that out there?" asked Dylan. "That's just what we do when we're messing around."

"Then let's mess around," said Elijah.

Michael smiled. "Yeah. I'm with you."

ELIJAH RECEIVED THE first pass and tossed it blindly to Michael, who was already in the middle of a short, looping run. He reached for the ball, turned one-eighty, and charged.

The Brute Force defense, which had grown accustomed to Team 16's weak, predictable patterns, backpedaled to fill the lane while Elijah shot forward, shouting "Switch! Switch it!"

Instantly Michael reversed the direction of their passing and fed Dylan, who just as quickly fed Elijah; three steps later, he buried the ball with an old-school two-handed dunk. The crowd erupted.

Thirteen to eleven.

On the next play, the ball lofted high toward Big Al's waving arms. It should have been an easy pass, but at the last minute,

Michael threw a hip at the giant, knocking him off balance. Elijah was right there to capitalize. He plucked the ball from the sky and faked a jumper. But instead of shooting, he slid it across to Dylan, who stood wide open by the two-point line.

"Oh shit!" said Skillz when he realized their mistake.

Dylan secured the pass, tucked his toes behind the white line, and buried the ball.

The score was tied at thirteen with less than a minute remaining. Quite possibly, the next team to score would be declared the winner.

42

ELIJAH'S MEMORY OF the rest of the game was etched in flashes of light and movement.

He remembered Dylan streaking across the court, pulling ahead of his man by an arm's length.

And in the microsecond of time that elapsed while the skinny white boy planted his right foot and launched, he saw his friend evolving, transcending his own game and becoming not just a better player but a different kind of player, a game changer. Dylan's body hung in space, filling Elijah's field of vision with outstretched arms and legs, a moving embodiment of athletic purpose, graceful and resolute. At the peak of Dylan's ascension, his arm hung behind him, trailing the ball. And finally, near the end of his flight, he swung that arm up and over his head, and slammed the ball home.

At the sound of the referee's whistle, the score was fourteen to thirteen; Team 16 had won Hoops.

"LET'S GO CELEBRATE," said Dylan.

"Yeah." Michael released his two friends from his bear hug long enough to examine their trophy. "What's the most expensive place in town? We could have a three-thousand-dollar dinner if we want."

Elijah pointed toward the parking lot; Sam Lehigh waited with his mother outside his generic blue rental. "I'll have to catch up with you guys in a little bit."

"What?" said Michael. "Can't we at least get a couple hours to celebrate as a team? Can't that dude wait?"

"I'm sorry," said Elijah. "He's got a plane to catch tonight. I'll come find you guys later. I swear."

"Fine." Michael forced out a smile. "You'd better call. I might be jealous as hell, but I still want to hear all about it."

"Me too," said Dylan. "Put in a good word for me, okay? I'm about to get my grades up."

"No, you ain't. Don't lie." Michael grabbed him by the shoulder and pulled him close. "Come on, man. Let Elijah do his thing."

ELIJAH'S MOTHER GREETED him first, wrapping her arms around him in a big hug. "I'm so proud of you." And then in a whisper, "You did the right thing, you know. I'm sure of it now."

"Thanks, Mom," he said.

Sam pumped Elijah's hand in a firm shake. "Hell of a game, son. A hell of a game. I think you've got a great future ahead of you. How about we go for dinner and talk about it?"

"Thank you, sir." The word *son* practically exploded in Elijah's head. He knew that certain men—coaches in particular—liked to use that term for anyone under the age of thirty. So it wasn't personal, any more than it was for him to say *sir*. But the word had knocked something loose inside him. Because wasn't this the time for his father to emerge from the crowd and acknowledge him?

It's me, Son, he was supposed to say. *I'm here, and I'm so proud of you.*

He knew how unlikely it was, but still . . . He searched one last time because he couldn't help himself. And then, for the time being, at least, he let it go. After all, there was a lot to be happy about. Team 16 had gone all the way. They'd won, and of that he was proud.

"I don't want to rush things." Sam checked his watch. "But I went ahead and made reservations at a steak house; I hope that's okay."

"Yes, sir." But Elijah was only half listening. A man by the chain-link fence was staring at him, and he was of the right height and skin tone. Broad-shouldered, possibly in his late thirties, but age was hard for Elijah to gauge. The man smiled and nodded, but just as quickly he took a call on his cell and walked away. *Could it be?*

"Excellent," said Sam. "Let's go."

43

SAM DROPPED ELIJAH and his mother off in the early evening with the promise that he'd return during the school season to watch him play again.

"We'll be in touch," he said. "And it goes without saying that we're very excited about the possibility of putting you in an orange jersey."

Elijah's mother hugged him again, but all he felt was a spasm of disappointment about the man who had smiled at him. Of course it hadn't been his father. Why had he ever thought his father was going to come see him play?

"Syracuse University," his mother said. "Can you believe it?"

He shook his head.

"But you know why I'm most proud of you?"

"Why?" he said.

"Because you and your friends took a stand today. You went out there dressed as yourselves, and you showed the whole world that you have integrity and can't be bought." She pulled back and regarded him with tear-filled eyes. "Today, Elijah, you've become a man. A strong man."

"Thanks, Mom."

Elijah set the brochures and folders Sam had given him on the kitchen counter. He checked his phone and saw, in addition to a voice mail from Michael (most likely telling him where they'd be meeting up), one brief text from Kerri.

"Got your cell number from my dad," the text said. "Hope that's okay. How was baseball?"

"Good," texted Elijah. "Want to go for some coffee?"

"If you still want to hear my plan," texted Kerri. "What's your address? I'll pick you up, but no jokes about my car."

"Okay." Michael's message would have to wait.

THE INSIDE OF the Fiat felt like a carnival ride designed for ten-year-olds. No matter how he adjusted the seat, Elijah's knees stuck up and into his chin. He sat folded in on himself, trying to make conversation.

"You look nice," he said.

"Thanks. Are you saying that out of politeness or because you really mean it?"

"Both, actually. Do you question everything?"

"Everything. Thank you for being polite, *and* for meaning it. I hate shopping, but I moved in such a hurry that I didn't even get a chance to pack. Most of my clothes are at my mother's house in Virginia." Kerri pushed a button above the rearview mirror; the roof slid back, letting in a flow of warm night air.

"Why did you move in a hurry?"

"My father would kill me if I told you." Kerri paused, considering. "Okay, you promise not to tell?"

"Promise."

"He had a minor heart attack. That's why he retired, and why I moved here so quickly. You've seen the way he takes care of himself?"

"The cigar-and-beer diet?"

"Right. So when he got out of the VA hospital, I talked it over with my mother and decided that he's the only father I'm ever going to have. If I'm going to try to have more of a relationship with him, it's got to be now."

"That's good of you."

"You know that he likes you, don't you?"

Elijah jerked his head in surprise. "I think you might be talking about a different person."

"It's true. Breaking up concrete, plates on the lawn mower, and all the other ridiculous chores. They're not really chores; he was testing you, trying to see what it would take to get you to quit."

Elijah extended his arm out the open roof. Despite his cramped position, it felt good to be driving with the top down, listening to this strange, frenetic girl. He felt as though he could listen to her talk forever. "How is that a sign of fondness? I was trying to help him out, not get into the Navy SEALs."

"Because that's the kind of person he is. It's also what he did for the army."

"So you're officially admitting he's not an accountant?"

Kerri smiled and rolled her eyes. "Not even close. His job was to train Special Forces guys for what's called 'unconventional warfare.' He had to test them and push them to their absolute limits to find their breaking point."

"Seriously?"

"Yes. And do you know what he did when he found their breaking point? He pushed them even farther. Most of the guys would break, of course."

"What does that even mean?"

"The breaking part? Means they'd give up, quit, or go crazy. But the few who made it . . . those were the men he'd assign to his team. And they'd go on special missions all over the world. Sometimes they'd go in so deep that they wouldn't even have support."

"Jesus! How do you know all this stuff?"

They arrived at a small coffee shop with plenty of outdoor tables. Inside, she stepped to the counter and ordered two cappuccinos with hardly a pause in their conversation. "Look, some girls are into shopping and makeup and catching the most popular guy; this is what I'm into. Though more specifically the criminology side of things. Is that too weird for you?"

"No, but you telling me that your father was trying to find my breaking point, that's weird. Speaking of which, what is that?" He pointed to her cup.

"It's just coffee and steamed milk. Try it."

They chose an outside table under the glow of a streetlamp. Elijah noticed Kerri's hands, which were especially slender and elegant; her nails were done in a two-tone of pink and off-white. He wondered if she'd painted them for him. He hoped so.

She scattered a handful of white plastic squares on the table. "Anyway, the whole point of coming here was so I could tell you about my plan."

"Right," said Elijah. "Your plan to take down the gang. But what are these?"

"GPS trackers that I stole from my father. The cheapest, most elegant solution to your problem. I found this whole box of surveillance stuff he had from work. We're going to use them as a counterinsurgency measure."

"I have no idea what that means." Elijah was getting the hang of drinking his cappuccino; he sipped so that he got three parts coffee to one part froth. "I'm pretty sure no one knows what that means."

"Then I shall explain," she said.

"Okay," said Elijah. "But my phone is buzzing like crazy. I need to answer it."

Elijah swiped his phone just as a second voice mail showed up on his screen, this one from Dylan's mother. Quickly he played Michael's message. His voice sounded wrong, too high-pitched, and panicked. "Elijah! Something's happened. You gotta call me right away."

The one from Dylan's mother was incomprehensible, borderline hysterical. At some point, a man took the phone from Dylan's mother and introduced himself as Detective Tillman. In a slow, deliberate voice, he asked Elijah to call the Baltimore Police Department as soon as possible.

Elijah's fingers shook as he pulled up Michael's number on his favorites tab.

"Elijah? Is that you?"

"It's me. What's going on?"

A pause. The drawing in of air. "Dylan's dead, man."

Elijah stopped breathing and counted off seconds.

One.

Two.

Three.

Four.

He knew what the words meant logically, but there was no way to accept it. How could Dylan be dead? They'd been playing ball together just a few hours before. It was impossible.

"Elijah, man, you there?"

"Yeah, I'm here." *That's not my voice,* he thought. *I don't sound like this. So who's talking?* "What are you telling me?"

"He's dead. Dylan's dead. We were walking home with the trophy, right?" Michael's words came slowly, haltingly.

Elijah tried to picture the two of them, one broad, with a swaggering gait, the other thin, bounding ahead on the balls of his feet.

Michael continued, sobbing freely, no longer trying to hold back. "We stopped outside my house and talked about what we were going to do with our share of the money. Dylan said he'd changed his mind about the Mustang 5.0 and wanted to buy a complete set of them X-Men comics. Like a first edition thing or something." He blew his nose. "And I was giving him crap about it, you know, because they're just, like, comic books."

"Tell me the rest." Again, with the voice that wasn't his.

"He got all hurt and offended and called me Fat Boy." A choking laugh laced with the edge of hysteria. "I felt bad, so I said I was sorry and hugged him. I told him he was my white brother and he could spend his money however he wanted. After that, man . . . I don't know."

"Tell me," said Elijah. "Exactly what happened. Come on."

"I went up the walkway to my house, and Dylan kept going. We were gonna get cleaned up and change, and then wait to hear from you. You know, to hear what the Syracuse guy had to say."

"And . . ."

"Somebody—somebody shot him," stammered Michael. "I was in my kitchen getting a bowl of cereal, and I heard a loud pop, but I figured it was just fireworks. You know, some kids setting off M-80s or something. I didn't think anything of it. But Dylan's neighbors found him lying on the sidewalk. Somebody shot him in his back, Elijah."

44

OF ALL THE possible responses to his friend's death, Elijah wouldn't have guessed silence. He sat rigid in the Fiat's passenger seat, gripping his phone tightly, as though he could squeeze the bad messages right out of it. When Kerri pulled up at his house, he tried to speak, but no words came to him.

"Can't you tell me what's wrong?" she asked.

He shook his head and staggered to his house.

Later, at the police station, Elijah's mother, Mrs. Henderson, and Mrs. Buchanan sat in the waiting room while the remaining sons met with Detectives Tillman and Stacey. Detective Tillman was bald and paunchy, wearing an ill-fitting suit, while Stacey was short and clean-shaven and had dark bags under his eyes. The boys sat next to each other in a small, private office containing a desk and four gray steel chairs.

"We'd like to ask you some questions about your friend Dylan," said Detective Tillman.

"You're going to find who did this?" asked Michael.

"Yes, but right now we're the ones who ask the questions. When was the last time you two saw Dylan?"

"At the end of the tournament," said Elijah. "I stayed, and he and Michael went home."

"In a car?" asked Detective Tillman.

"We walked," said Michael.

After they went through the details and specifics of the walk home, the detectives ran through a litany of other questions.

"Did Dylan have any known enemies?"

"No," said Michael.

"Was he in a gang?"

"No."

"Did he deal or use drugs?"

"No."

Michael started to get a dangerous look in his eyes, so Elijah took over and spoke for both of them. He answered every question and told them about Money and the Blood Street Nation. He answered honestly, describing his encounters in the black Mercedes word for word. Encounters that he hadn't shared with Michael before. Yet every question he answered prompted three more. It didn't take long for him to see that the detectives didn't believe him.

Tillman: How did you meet this guy, Money, and what's his real name?

Elijah: I don't know his real name. He was watching me play a pickup game at the Battlegrounds. He called me over to his car.

Stacey: What do you mean you don't know his real name? He bought you four-hundred-dollar sneakers and sponsored your team, and you're telling me you didn't get his name?

Tillman: That's strange. Does that sound strange to you, Ken?

Stacey: A little, Bob. What did he look like, Elijah?

Elijah: Shaved head, brown eyes, maybe five-feet-eight. He wore a black hoodie and jeans.

Tillman: Skin color?

Elijah: Like mine. [*Holds out his forearm for them to see.*]

Stacey: And you said he had a gun? Know what kind of a gun?

Elijah: I don't know. It was silver. [*Holds his fingers apart eight inches.*] This big.

Tillman: And tell us again why you didn't report that encounter?

Elijah: Because he had a picture of my mother. He had the addresses of where she works. He told me to keep my mouth shut and not tell anyone about him. He said if I was smart and followed directions, no one would get hurt. I believed him.

Stacey: Did he directly threaten you or your mother? You say he's dangerous, but I'm not getting it, so help me understand.

Elijah [*starting to crack*]: Okay. I'll spell it out for you. This guy, Money, shot my friend in the back. That's what makes him dangerous. Get it now? [*Standing up, voice rising.*] I mean, why are you wasting time talking to us? Why aren't you out looking for Money?

Tillman: Because we've got some more questions—

Michael slammed his fist on the desk; the massive metal slab—that must have dated back to the Second World War—shuddered from the impact. "Enough. We told you what we know. Now we're going home."

"Leave your phones with us," said Tillman. "We need to look at all your calls and texts."

"I don't have it with me," said Michael.

"Go home and get it," said Stacey.

Elijah fished his from his back pocket, noticing for the first time that he'd cracked the casing from squeezing it so hard. It clattered onto the metal desk.

The two boys met their worried, grief-stricken mothers in the waiting room, along with Mrs. Buchanan, who hadn't wanted to be alone. They took a minivan cab home; several blocks from Elijah's house, Dylan's mother looked out the window and said, "He's not dead, you know."

"I'm sorry, dear." Elijah's mother covered the woman's hands with her own. "I'm so very sorry."

"It's a mistake," said Mrs. Buchanan. "He's coming home later. He always comes home. I'm going to leave the door unlocked and make his favorite meal for dinner. And he's going to come home."

"What was his favorite meal?" asked Elijah's mother.

"Lasagna and garlic bread. That was his favorite." And then the spell was broken. Mrs. Buchanan let the tears come. "He's gone, isn't he?"

The cabdriver pulled up in front of Elijah's house and had the decency not to interrupt. After a few minutes that seemed like an eternity, Mrs. Henderson touched Elijah's mother on the arm and said, "Go on home with Elijah. I'll take care of her."

ELIJAH PACED THE KITCHEN, unable to look at his mother. It was three a.m.

"Tell me this has nothing to do with that gang," she said.

"I don't know, Mom. It probably does." He wanted to punch holes in the walls. He wanted to go back to Banks's house and tear down his shed but this time use his bare hands and not ropes and a winch. What else could he destroy? Not what, but who.

His mother covered her face with her hands and then took a deep breath. "Son, we've got to leave this place."

"What?" He wanted to finish his last thought, about who he could destroy. Because there was someone, wasn't there? Someone who drove a black Mercedes and carried a small silver gun in the front pocket of his hoodie. Elijah wondered how badly he could beat Money without going to jail. Could he beat him within an inch of his life, or possibly all the way? He was surprised at how comfortable the idea felt. It wasn't at all scary.

"We have to get out of here." She talked more to herself than him. "I don't even know what I'm doing anymore; it's like I'm acting out a role from someone else's life." She pulled her address book from a drawer and flipped the pages. "As soon as I make arrangements, we're moving, Elijah. You'll have to finish your senior year in a new school."

"Hold on, Mom." Her words were beginning to filter through the newly forming blossom of rage. He didn't want to talk and plan. What if he calmed down? What would he be left with, a dead friend and a lump of guilt metastasizing inside him like a tumor?

"I can't even begin to think about my responsibility in this right now," she said. "Because first we're going to get somewhere safe. Do you understand?"

Elijah wanted to say no, that he couldn't think about moving right now. He wanted to tell her that she was wrong, and that running away wasn't the answer. He was supposed to do something. Get out there and find Money. Even Banks would agree; after all, what was the point of all his crazy chores and lessons? Think, find the enemy's weak point, and then act; that was what he needed to do.

But there was something about his mother's voice . . . steely but brittle. He thought about Mrs. Buchanan, and the strange, flat way she'd talked. *It's a mistake. He's coming home later. He always comes home.* That was how a mother spoke after she'd lost her son.

Elijah went to his room and tried not to scream or smash his fists against his bedroom wall. He did sets of push-ups until his arms gave out and he collapsed. He lay like that for a long time, soaked in sweat, his tears collecting on the hardwood floor, until sleep claimed him.

45

MICHAEL CAME BY the next morning, and they walked to the bank to cash the check from the tournament. They used three hundred of it to buy suits for Dylan's funeral—charcoal with light pinstripes, a trio of black buttons, inexpensive but not tacky. They also bought new white shirts and ties, all picked from the clearance rack at Burlington. Another fifty got them a new NCAA replica ball—since Dylan's had been confiscated as evidence.

At the food court, Elijah stared at his Coke, of which he hadn't taken a sip. "I can't stop thinking about it."

"Me neither," said Michael. "I can't sleep. Every time I try, I see him. You know, wearing them big baggy clothes and flashing that crazy grin. Pissed off at me because I bagged on his X-Men comics."

Elijah knew it was something he was supposed to smile at, but his smiles were gone. "I keep going over all the stuff that's happened in the last month. It's like, if I can only figure out what I could have done differently . . ."

"What? Like not taking them stupid shoes?" Michael put a massive hand over his eyes and held it there. "That was me, re-member? I got those shoes. If it wasn't for me, Dylan would be running around right now in his broke old Adidas. I might as well have pulled the trigger."

Elijah watched his friend cry silently. He made no move to stop him or correct his damning words. He didn't agree, but it would have taken too much effort to dissuade him, and he was tired. So he said nothing.

When Michael removed his hand and wiped his nose, he looked like a different person. Older. Serious. He didn't have his usual confidence and swagger, and his eyes were heavy and sad. "What are we supposed to do now?"

"Right now we've got to help Dylan's mother plan a funeral so we can say goodbye to our friend."

"Okay, man. I'll try. You just tell me what to do, and I'll try to do it."

AN HOUR LATER, they stood with their packages outside Mrs. Buchanan's house. Michael had gone silent; he shifted nervously on his big feet, rivulets of sweat running down the sides of his face. "I can't do this, man. I'm sorry."

Elijah grabbed him firmly by the shoulder, steadying him.

Michael looked down. "I just can't do it. I got to go."

"You have to do this. Dylan would do it for you, and you know it."

Michael lowered his head onto Elijah's shoulder and wrapped his arms around his friend. Elijah hugged him back, feeling very much like they were hanging on for dear life. After what seemed like a long time, Michael broke free and shuffled away, muttering.

"I'm sorry," said Michael. "I gotta get out of here."

"Don't do this, man," said Elijah. "It's not right. You can't just walk away."

Mrs. Buchanan opened the door while dabbing at her streaking makeup with a tissue.

"Hello, Mrs. Buchanan," Elijah said.

"Do you want to come in?" She held the door open for him and then said, in a voice that was almost a whisper, "I'm sorry for the things I said yesterday. In the cab. I know he's dead."

"I'm sorry," said Elijah.

"I just thought, Dylan was always out at school or playing basketball. Maybe it was a mistake and he was still out playing, and sooner or later, he'd come home."

Elijah nodded. "He loved you."

"He did. Dylan had such a kind heart. He was never angry like his brother, Marvin."

"How is Marvin taking it?" asked Elijah.

"He says he's fine, but I don't ever really know what it's like for him in that place. I think he tells me things are fine so it will be easier for me. All you boys are like that. You don't want to upset us, but then look what happens."

She said more, and Elijah tried to listen attentively. But really he was thinking of how strange it was to hear his friend talked about in the past tense. One day had elapsed, and it was *Dylan used to . . .*

"It's my fault." She looked away from him, at a spot on the far wall. "For making him take off that jersey. I should have known there'd be some kind of payback. That's one thing I learned from Marvin's troubles—there's always payback. You know that, don't you, Elijah?"

Elijah looked into her eyes and saw no trace of anger, only sadness. He nodded because he didn't trust himself to speak.

"He always looked up to you, you know," she said. "He wanted to be like you."

Elijah said he was sorry, but try as he might, he couldn't explain *why*. Because to do that would have required him to go beyond the senselessness of her son's death and into the realm of culpability. Because he had put Dylan in danger. If he'd accepted the shoes and jerseys (and whatever strings had come along with them), his friend would be alive. Gang affiliated, maybe, but alive.

At the door, Mrs. Buchanan's hug was tentative, as though she might be able to stave off the funeral if only Elijah would stay a little longer. "I'm so glad you came. It means a lot to me."

"I have to go," he said. "My mother's waiting for me."

"Thank her for the flowers," she said. "And the food that she brought over. Tell her it was sweet but that I haven't been able to eat."

On his way out the door, he handed her an envelope with the remaining Hoops money, more than two and a half thousand dollars. "This is to help with the funeral costs."

"I'll give it to Dylan's father; he's taking care of the funeral arrangements." She kissed him on his check. "Thank you for being Dylan's friend. He loved you and Michael. He really did. You boys meant the world to him."

46

THE FUNERAL WAS UNBEARABLE, an endless succession of sweating, nicely dressed people, none of whom seemed to have known Dylan well at all. Or at least, that was how it seemed from the things they said in the church. *He was a good brother. He was a dedicated student. A proud member of the church.* Elijah wanted to go up and set the record straight, but for whom? He had a feeling that the false words were exactly the ones people wanted to hear. Needed to hear. So they could put the whole thing into a category and move on. Get into their cars and say, *He was such a good boy. What a tragedy! So sad.* But it wasn't that straightforward, and Mrs. Buchanan's words weighed heavily on him: *There's always payback. You know that, don't you?*

Later, after he'd kissed and hugged and said goodbye to countless mothers, aunts, and cousins, Elijah wandered through his neighborhood, sweating through his suit. More words echoed in his head. *He loved you and Michael. You meant the world to him.*

He looked at the perfect front yards he'd passed so many times before, but they looked different now. False. Their promise of safety and happiness was an illusion, because good kids like Dylan, and Ray Shiver, had been sacrificed. And for what?

He stopped in front of a remote-control dune buggy that a kid had forgotten on his front sidewalk. For some inexplicable reason, Elijah was tempted to step on it. Smash it to bits. He raised his leg but hesitated.

What are you doing? You need to get a grip.

He stepped over the toy and began jogging toward Banks's house. Four days had passed since he'd last been there, but the driveway was exactly as he'd left it, half-covered in pavers. The remaining pallets were untouched, as was the pile of mason's sand. He nudged the sand with his toe, wondering if he'd get to finish the job before moving. He wanted to, if for no other reason than to see what it looked like.

Elijah took off his jacket and thumped some pavers to the ground in a loose circle before he got down on his knees. The sand's heat worked through his thin dress pants. He laid down the pavers and tapped them into place with the mallet. He dropped another ten from the pallet and increased his pace, until his shirt and pants were soaked through with sweat.

In between sets, he carried the few remaining concrete chunks into the backyard. He strained under their weight until his breathing became short. His pants were torn from the jagged edges of the concrete blocks. His shirt stuck to his skin except for where he had rolled the sleeves up; in these spots his forearms were laced with cuts and abrasions, which he didn't feel or notice.

"Hey," said Banks, half hanging out the back screen door. "What are you doing?"

"What's it look like?" Elijah picked up the last chunk. It was far too big and heavy to carry, which is why he'd left it in the first place. He staggered under the weight, and dropped it.

Banks jammed his feet into a pair of sneakers. "It looks like you're acting a little nuts. And why are you wearing a suit? Hey, I'm talking to you."

"I've been at church." It occurred to him that Banks didn't know about Dylan.

"Good for you," said Banks. "Maybe you should go back to church and talk to Pastor Fredericks."

Elijah said nothing.

Banks tried a different approach. "You said you needed two days off for your tournament. Do you know how many days you missed?"

Elijah shook his head.

"Four," said Banks. "That means you broke our deal. We're done."

"Fine." Elijah knelt in the sand next to the giant chunk. He levered it up against his thighs and staggered another ten feet before dropping it again.

"Hey." Banks moved a little closer and put a hand on his shoulder. "There's no second or third chances in my world."

"I said fine. I'm just going to move this last piece." Elijah grunted and strained, sliding the piece up his thighs and back into a carrying position. He made it three steps before dropping it.

"Go home," said Banks. "You want to cripple yourself, do it someplace else."

Elijah got down on his knees and tried to position the piece for another lift. "Just leave me alone." Concrete dust stuck to the sweat on his arms, legs, and back.

"Listen," said Banks. "I know you've got some problems . . ."

Problems. His friend was dead, and his other friend was involved with the gang that had killed him. He didn't know what to do or who to turn to, and his mother was threatening to move them to another state. He was dangerously close to tears, but there was no way he was going to let Banks see him cry. "You don't know anything about me."

"That's right," said Banks. "I don't know anything about you or anyone else. I didn't ask for this. I told your mother I was no good with kids, that I'd make a lousy mentor, but she wouldn't listen."

"Mentor? Who needs a mentor? I came here to work. To help you." Elijah pulled himself to sitting, arms resting on his knees. Heat came off him in waves, and he felt like he might explode. He stood up and hustled away, down the half-finished driveway. Kerri called after him once, carrying his jacket, but he kept running.

HE DECIDED IT was time for action, because a fire was burning inside him. But what should he do? His mother couldn't help him; her answer was to move away and pretend like nothing had happened. Start over again. Elijah understood her reasons, but he couldn't pretend. Just like he couldn't pretend anymore that his father was going to come back. It was time for him to grow up and take action. But how?

Find the breaking point, and then push.

What was Money's breaking point? Arrogance, maybe. But you couldn't push on arrogance; it wasn't a tangible thing, like the corner studs of a dilapidated old shed. Banks couldn't help him. All he wanted to do was hide out and drink his crappy lime beer and smoke cigars. *Screw him,* Elijah thought.

But maybe Banks did know a thing or two. Because he *had* jacked up that thug at the diner. It was like he'd known exactly what to do, and then had gone and done it. No thinking. No worrying. No deliberating or second-guessing. That's how Elijah wanted to solve his problems with Money and BSN.

Think. There's got to be a weak point.

He thought back to his second meeting with Money. *You wouldn't want to disrespect me because I have a gun?* That told him a lot about Money. *He* respected the gun. Which meant that he also feared it. So there it was, whether Elijah liked it or not. He needed to get a gun. That was how the world worked. It was what he had to do in order to protect his mother and avenge his friend.

Harold's words echoed in his head: *If you want to get a piece for protection, I can hook you up.*

47

ELIJAH'S LAST STOP of the day was at Joe's Texas Hots. He made a quick attempt at smoothing his clothes and stepped in line behind a young family with two boys. The parents were trying to place their order, but the littlest one wasn't cooperating. "Do you want a hot dog? Do you want french fries? Lemonade? Take that pacifier out and use your words." The boy shook his head at every question, eyes wide with his own obstinacy. His older brother, who couldn't have been more than six or seven years old, held a small blue rubber basketball with a red Hawks logo on it. He stood off by himself, trying to spin it on his finger; the ball got away from him and bounced into Elijah's feet.

Elijah picked it up. The ball was so small, he could almost hide it inside his palm. Without thinking, he spun it onto his finger and gave it a couple of swipes to speed it up. It became a blue-and-red blur. Elijah felt the father's eyes on him, watching him closely, judging him. It was a protective thing, Elijah knew. A good thing. He wanted to pull the man aside and say, *Keep doing that. . . . Don't ever stop watching out for him. Don't stop trying to keep him safe, because someday he's going to need your help, and you've got to be there, or else . . .* But he said nothing. Instead, he knelt down on the tile floor and called the boy over.

"Here you go, buddy." Slowly he transferred the spinning ball onto the boy's finger.

"Awesome." The boy watched it spinning, mesmerized. "Look, Dad!"

"Thanks," said the father reluctantly.

"No problem."

When it was his turn to order, he asked the girl at the counter if Harold was working.

She might have been pretty, but Elijah had no more room for such things. Besides, she was so hopelessly bored that it seemed a struggle for her to keep her eyelids open. "He's on break." With effort, she lifted her arm and pointed toward the outdoor patio, and then droned, "I can take the next customer."

Harold sat at a picnic table in the far corner of the patio with a tray of food. Like before, he wore a white cook's shirt with a green apron, and he sipped from a monstrous cup of soda.

"Hey, Harold." Elijah walked over and took a seat opposite.

"My man Elijah. I'm sorry to hear about your boy Dylan. You want me to get you a dog or some fries? It's free when I'm working."

"No thanks. I'm not hungry."

"When my cousin passed, I didn't eat nothing for a week. Lost ten pounds, and I'm already mad skinny."

"Do you remember the last time I was here, when I got into a beef with that guy?"

"Yeah, Bull. He come after you?"

"No, but you mentioned something about protection."

"Yeah, I remember."

"Did you mean it?"

"Depends," said Harold. "You gonna go after whoever hurt Dylan?"

"Yeah, that's exactly what I'm going to do."

"Good, 'cause I always liked that boy. He didn't deserve that.

Cops won't do nothing, either, so it comes down to you anyway. All we got's each other, right?" Harold's hot dog disappeared in small, quick bites. "What kind of a piece you want?"

"I don't even know." Elijah looked at his dirty, scratched-up hands and tried to imagine holding a gun. "Something small and easy to carry. I've got two hundred bucks. Is that enough?"

Harold nodded. "Come back tomorrow. Bring the money, and I'll hook you up."

"Thanks, Harold. Thanks for helping me."

"No problem."

48

ELIJAH WENT STRAIGHT home and took the longest shower of his life. He watched the bottom of the tub as water flowed off him in brown streams of dirt, sweat, and dust. When it started to run clear, he used soap and shampoo, and then closed his eyes. He focused on the sensation of the water drumming on his skin, and the steam that enveloped him. For the first time since Dylan's death, he breathed deeply and easily. Inside him, a plan was forming.

He lay down on his bed and remembered back to a time when Dylan, Michael, and he had been in the fourth grade. Elijah had been playing in games at the Battlegrounds for several months, but this was the first time all three boys had been allowed.

"Did you see me out there?" asked Michael. "I was on fire. I'm gonna be playing here every day, until I go on to the pros."

"Of course I seen you," said Dylan. "You're the biggest nine-year-old in Baltimore. The dude in the traffic copter seen you. Everybody seen you; that doesn't mean you got skills."

"Everybody know I got skills," said Michael. "But keep being a hater and watch me take your birthday present back to the damn store. Me and Elijah will come to your party empty-handed."

Dylan studied his friend to see if he was serious. "Okay, I'm sorry. You played good."

"That's right," said Michael. "And you ain't gonna believe the present we bought. In a million years you couldn't guess what it is."

"Come on, guys." Dylan bounced around his two friends like a terrier. "You can tell me, and I'll act surprised when I get it. No one will know. Is it that model rocket? Or them packets of space ice cream that freeze up when you open them?"

In the end Dylan had waited. The present: an official Wilson NCAA replica ball that had cost them twenty-nine dollars plus tax.

ELIJAH'S PHONE—WHICH HE'D gotten back from Detective Tillman and had taped back together again—pinged with a string of messages from Kerri:

"Hi, it's me. About my father: he didn't know your friend was killed. I'm so sorry, Elijah."

"Hi. Kerri again. I know you probably want to be alone, but call me."

"Last message, I promise. I don't know you well enough to say that I'm worried about you, but I am. Please call, just to let me know you're okay, even though I know you're not okay."

She was right, he was not okay. And what difference did it make if Banks hadn't known? He was still an asshole, because Elijah had worked hard for him and deserved to be treated better. He wasn't in the army, and neither was Banks. Screw him. As for Kerri, he didn't want to hear any more about her plan. He had his own plan, and it didn't involve GPS tracking devices or taking down a whole gang. His plan involved a gun and getting rid of a piece of human garbage that went by the name of Money.

49

THE NEXT MORNING, Elijah pulled on jeans and a T-shirt and dialed Michael's cell.

"Where are you?" asked Elijah.

"Home." Michael's voice came in a whisper. Flat. "Since the funeral, all I've been doing is sleeping and watching TV."

"I need to meet with your friend Money."

"He ain't my friend."

"Whatever," said Elijah. "Are you going to help me or not?"

An edge came into Michael's voice. "Is that why you called? To bust my balls again? To make me feel guilty?"

"I told you, I called to get Money's number. That's all."

Silence.

"Michael, did you hear me?"

"Yeah, I heard you. Why you want to talk to him? You want to get yourself shot, too?"

"That's my own business, just like it was yours to get us a sponsor who shot our friend." He knew it was a cruel thing to say, but he felt like being cruel. He also felt like Michael deserved it. Besides, it was true.

"We don't know that Money killed him. Could have been any

number of people in the Nation, acting out an order. Could be the same one that shot Ray Shiver."

"Like who?"

"I don't know," said Michael. "Could be anyone. Besides, you won't be able to find Money unless he wants to be found. Think, man. You don't know his real name. You don't know where he lives. All you got is a young brother in a dark hoodie."

"I saw his face."

"Okay, so you seen his face. Big deal."

"Look, are you going to give me his number or not?"

"He won't recognize you when it comes up on his phone. He won't answer."

"Then I'll use your phone."

"Man, I ain't—"

"I'll be at your house in an hour."

Elijah grabbed his keys and the stack of twenties from his sock drawer that he'd earned working for Banks. He tried to brush past his mother with a quick kiss on her cheek.

"Where are you going?" she asked.

"Michael's. Be back soon."

"When you get back, we need to talk about moving."

He waited by the door for her to finish.

"I called my cousin in Buffalo, and she heard about a job for me. She says there's a good magnet school you could go to. They have a basketball team, too."

Elijah nodded.

"Soon, Elijah," she said. "I'm serious about this."

"Okay," he said.

THE DEAL TOOK less than ten minutes and was conducted in an alley, behind Joe's Texas Hots.

"See that?" said Harold. "That's the safety. And here's how the clip goes in. You got it?"

The gun was a Hi-Point 9mm, known for being cheap, easy to conceal, and highly reliable, or so Harold said. Numbers and manufacturing stamps had been filed off, and Harold had wrapped the whole thing in a red-and-white-checked kitchen rag, which Elijah stuffed into the bottom of his backpack. Included was a twenty box of Starfire rounds.

"Got it," said Elijah. They stood between a blue steel Dumpster and the grease pit, talking in a low whisper. It felt heavier than he'd expected. At the same time, it looked too much like a toy. He wondered how something that looked like a toy could shoot holes in people.

"Most people run away if they see a gun," said Harold. "But if they don't, and you have to use it . . . aim lower than you think you should. Because it'll kick up."

"Okay," said Elijah, only half paying attention. His thoughts raced ahead to the rest of his plan. Getting Money to meet him. The confrontation. And then what?

"Be careful," said Harold. "And remember . . ."

"I know," said Elijah. "I didn't get it from you."

"No," said Harold. "You don't even know me."

51

OUTSIDE MICHAEL'S HOUSE, Elijah knocked once and let himself in. Michael was in the living room, watching a Cavaliers game on television.

"My moms and sisters are out," said Michael. "So we can talk if you want to." A television tray held a bowl of Doritos and two glasses of Coke. "My moms put this out for you. I told her not to bother, but she said you're like family, which is funny because it's starting to feel like brother against brother. Man, why are you acting like this? Ain't we still friends?"

"I don't know how else to be." Elijah sat down next to Michael. They watched the game for a few minutes, LeBron James picking the other team apart play by play.

"You ever hear from the Syracuse guy, what's his name?"

"Sam Lehigh. Yeah. He's setting up a visit for me and my mom."

"Cool. That means they want you. You go out there, and they'll buy you a steak dinner, take you to watch a game. Probably let you sit with the team. You're going, right?"

"I don't know. Maybe. My mom wants to move to Buffalo."

"What? Like, faraway Buffalo, where it snows?"

"Yeah. We've got family there, but I don't remember them."

"When?"

"She says soon. As in a couple of weeks soon. She says it's not safe here anymore."

"Maybe it ain't. But you ain't gonna just pack up and leave, are you?"

"I know. I don't want to go." The silence between them became unbearable. "Are you going to let me use your phone?"

"It ain't a good idea, Elijah. I'm saying that as a friend."

"A friend would be helping me with this. Why don't you want to find out who killed Dylan?"

"I do, man. I really do, but . . ."

"But what?" Elijah stood and paced the floor.

"It's complicated."

"I'll bet it is." He stood over Michael, glaring, his anger blossoming again inside him. "So let me simplify it for you. If you don't give me your phone, I'll take it from you, and I don't care what I have to do to get it."

Silence. Elijah had never threatened his friend before. It felt strange, but it also felt justified.

"Go on," Elijah added. "Try me."

"Here." Michael pulled out his phone and scrolled through his contacts until he found the listing for M$. "You sure you know what you're doing?"

"No, but I'm going to do it anyway," said Elijah.

Michael pushed the call icon and handed the phone to Elijah. It rang and rang.

AFTER WHAT SEEMED like an eternity, a soft, flat voice on the other end of the line said, "What you want?"

"This is Elijah."

A pause. "And I said, what do you want?"

"We've got to talk."

"We're talking now," said Money.

"In person," said Elijah.

"Fine. You at Big Boy's?"

"Who's Big Boy?"

"Michael. I call him Big Boy, because of his size, right."

"Yeah, I'm at his house."

"Be ready, then." The line went dead.

ELIJAH AND MICHAEL waited in the driveway by the hoop they used to play under as little boys. The net had long since rotted away, and the rim was badly bent. Michael kicked at a cheap rubber ball that was half deflated. "You ain't doing nothing crazy, are you?" said Michael.

Elijah shrugged, feeling the weight of the gun on the shoulder straps of his backpack.

"You know you're the only real friend I got."

They both watched the Mercedes stop at the front of the house.

"Mrs. Buchanan said we should visit Dylan's grave," said Elijah. "If we want to."

"Okay," said Michael. "I'll go."

52

MONEY SILENTLY NAVIGATED through the streets of Elijah's neighborhood. It looked different from his vantage point in the passenger seat. The fronts of houses that had seemed so quaint and perfect now seemed like the thinnest of veneers. He thought that if he touched one, his finger would go right through the bricks or the wooden clapboards, because whatever goodness was there was fake, or too fragile to endure.

"You got something to say?" Money steered with one hand, touching his silver hoop earring with the other.

Elijah's backpack was tucked safely between his feet. Anytime he wanted, he could pull the gun out and give Money what he deserved. "Yeah. Why'd you kill my friend?"

Money sucked his teeth. "Man, what you don't know could fill a library. I didn't shoot nobody."

"I don't believe you. I saw you at the game." He mimicked Money's shooting gesture.

"I was just delivering a message from the boss to let you fools know just how bad you screwed up. I didn't do the deed, though; I'm past the dirty work. The boss got other people to do it."

"Who?"

"Man, I ain't here to answer questions. Get the information yourself."

Right. Elijah lifted the pack onto his lap. "What are you here for, then?"

"Business. That's what it's all about anyway. Money and business. They both the same."

They drove past the Battlegrounds and then east, past pawnshops, liquor stores, and bail bondsman's offices. Two shirtless boys chased a third on a bicycle; they caught him and knocked him off, then fought with each other over who would get to ride next.

"Look," said Money, pointing out the tinted windows at the poverty and decay, which seemed to worsen with each block.

"I see it."

"Yeah, what do you see?"

"A mess. Garbage. Graffiti."

"What else?"

Elijah looked straight ahead at the dashboard, not in the mood for Money's game.

"I'll tell you: it's where folks come to die. See 'em shuffling along, all sick and hungry and spent? See that dude on the stoop there, in the fake leather jacket next to his cart? Guess how old he is."

"I don't know. Fifty. Sixty."

Money pushed air through his teeth in the wheezy approximation of a laugh. "He's twenty-eight, four years older than me. We went to high school together."

"That's a shame." Elijah fiddled with the zipper of his pack. He opened it an inch, then two. "But in your own words, who cares?"

"You ought to, because every one of them is hungry for what you got."

"What I have right now is a dead friend."

"No, man. What you got is a chance. They pissed their chances away, but you still got yours. So here it is. I'm gonna tell you what happened to your friend, and you better learn something from it. Ready?"

"Okay."

"You guys screwed up. You dissed the Nation, and someone had to pay. That's the rule. It's always been the rule, and everyone on this street knows it. Even those kids back there with the bike. You mess up, and somebody's got to bleed."

"I get it, rule of the streets and all that. But Dylan had nothing to do with it."

"You think that matters, but it don't. It ain't that personal like that. Boss decided and gave an order. Somebody carried out that order and capped him. Simple as that."

"And you didn't cap anybody."

"Exactly." Money pulled up to a meter in front of an abandoned KFC; a trio of laconic thugs seemed to recognize the car. They smiled and gave the thug equivalent of a wave, a kind of combination lopsided grimace and shoulder shrug.

"I still don't believe you," said Elijah.

"Nobody cares what you believe, unless you can back it up." Money slid his gun out of the front pocket of his hoodie. "Can you back it up? Do you want to?"

Elijah pulled the zipper the rest of the way. He looked into the pack and saw the red-and-white-checked rag. He wasn't sure if he could do it, but he'd try. For Dylan. He would take out the Hi-Point and flip the safety off—just like Harold had showed him in the back alley—and shoot. A single report that would make his ears ring. Then what? His friend's murderer would be dead, which would be something. Unless Money was telling the truth and he wasn't the shooter. Was that even possible?

Possible, which meant that Elijah wasn't sure any longer, and his plan was crap.

He thought back to the lesson Banks had tried to teach him with the shed—bring the whole thing down on itself, without getting hurt. Inflict maximum damage with minimum risk. Shooting Money did not fit that criterion, because firing a gun hurt Elijah in a number of ways, like obliterating his chances of going to college (in favor of prison), and disappointing his mother. Measured in Banks's terms, he was on the verge of making a terrible mistake.

Money smiled. "Relax, man. I'm just messing around with you. The only shoot-outs you gonna be doing is on the hardwood at some Big Ten college, right? And that's cool, because it's part of the plan. So be smart. Your friend got smoked, but lots of people around here get smoked. Life's hard, but it keeps going, you know what I mean?"

"No." Elijah let the backpack slide down between his feet. "That makes no sense. You're not wise or even smart. But you know what? I'm going to find out who killed Dylan, and then I'm going to find out who you work for."

"And what are you gonna do then?" asked Money. "Assuming you can find that out, which you can't."

"You'll see." In fact, he had no idea. He didn't know how to bring down a gang or seek justice for his friend. He was a boy trying to be a man, and he felt as though he was failing.

"So it's like that, huh?" Money unlocked the doors.

"Guess so."

"Then maybe you should start watching your back. Be a shame if something happened to you before you get your shot at wearing the orange."

Elijah gritted his teeth, but one of the thugs tapped on the window, meeting his eyes with a steady glare. He shouldered his pack and got out. The long walk home took him back past the abandoned grocery carts, overflowing garbage cans, and broken forty-ounce bottles. Torn-up lottery and scratch tickets littered the sidewalks like a kind of confetti of lost hope, and the world's oldest twenty-eight-year-old—the one from Money's school days— peeled back his upper lip in a crooked, rotten-toothed grin.

ELIJAH COULD NOT believe his stupidity. The thought of having a gun in his house made him sick; he contemplated giving it back to Harold but in the end settled on a Dumpster behind a Dollar Store. After wiping the gun down with the checkered cloth—something he probably didn't need to do but had seen a hundred times on TV—he lifted the black plastic lid and let the gun disappear. Then he went home and locked himself in his bedroom. He turned off his phone and willed himself not to think about Dylan anymore.

Let the past be the past.

Which meant what? Moving to Buffalo and starting up in a new school? Maybe that was better than staying. He wouldn't have to deal with Michael anymore, or hear people talking about Blood Street Nation. Nor would he have to face Coach Walters and explain what had happened to Dylan.

In his closet he took out the orange Nike box and put it into his backpack, along with a lighter and a six-ounce bottle of his mother's nail polish remover. He walked to the Battlegrounds parking lot, where he found an almost empty steel garbage can. The acetone in the remover smelled sweet. It splashed, clear, over the shoes but went up in a small yellow-orange fireball that continued to burn inside the can long after Elijah walked away.

AFTER ELIJAH SPENT two more days in his bedroom, his mother knocked on his door and said, "There's someone here to see you."

"Who?" he called out.

"Get up out of that bed," she said, "and go find out. You've been in this room long enough."

Elijah dragged himself down the hall, muttering. He made a short mental list of people he did not want to see, in order of descending unpleasantness: Money. Bull. Michael. Banks. Kerri. He decided that the last one wasn't fair; Kerri wasn't at all unpleasant. On the contrary, he'd thought about her a lot. He just didn't want to talk to her right now. He didn't want to talk to anyone.

Banks stood on the opposite side of the door, looking as grave as ever. "Elijah," he said. "Can we talk?"

"What do you want?" said Elijah.

"I didn't know about your friend," said Banks. "I'm sorry. I read about it in the news, but I didn't put it together. Honestly, I'm sorry."

Elijah nodded but said nothing.

"Still, I shouldn't have talked that way to you. I'm terrible with people."

It was as much of a conciliatory gesture as Elijah thought he'd ever get from someone like Banks. He decided to take it. "It's okay."

"Do the police have any leads?" asked Banks.

"No." Elijah joined Banks on the stoop and sat on the top step. "I called them yesterday. They said they've been investigating, but none of the neighbors heard or saw anything. Except the gunshot."

"Typical." Banks sat next to him but looked straight ahead while he talked. "People are cowardly. They don't ever want to get involved."

"I guess," said Elijah.

"I lost friends," said Banks. "In the army. Everyone says things to try to help you with it, so you can accept it. But sometimes it's just plain unacceptable. Especially when it's a young person."

Elijah glanced over at him. "How did your friends die?"

"Different ways, but all violent. Shot. Blown up. Suicide." Banks picked distractedly at a callus on the palm of his hand. "Casualties of Iraq and Afghanistan. Tora Bora."

"What did you do?" asked Elijah. "Afterward, I mean. How did you deal with it?"

"Same thing I do now. I drank beer, smoked cigars, and had lots of bad dreams." Banks picked harder at his hand, and then closed it in a fist. Slowly he peeled back thumb and fingers until it was a palm again. "How are you dealing with it?"

"I've been sleeping a lot. And thinking. Being angry, too. My mom wants to move us to Buffalo because she thinks it'll be safer. Some suburb called Williamsville."

"I wish I knew what to tell you to make it better," said Banks. "But I don't. I'm forty-five years old, and I haven't figured it out. Maybe moving makes sense. I don't know."

"You still have bad dreams?" asked Elijah.

"Every night," said Banks.

"What did you really do in the army?"

Banks took a deep breath. "I was in Special Forces. Green Berets."

Elijah nodded. After several moments of silence, he said, "It's fine that you don't want to talk about it. I won't ask. By the way, you need a new blade on your table saw."

"What?" asked Banks.

"The project you're working on in your basement. The teeth

on your blade are dull and covered in pitch; it's why your wood keeps binding. You need to buy a new blade, and also lower it so the teeth are a touch higher than the board."

Banks looked at him, puzzled. "How do you know all that?"

"I told you, I've taken three years of tech classes. Checking the blade is the first thing we ever learned. It's like making sure there's gas in a lawn mower."

"I'll give that a try." He reached into his pocket and then set the Special Forces medallion on the steps between them. "I haven't forgotten our deal, you know. You're more than halfway through the list."

Elijah smiled and pushed the coin back toward Banks. "Start again tomorrow?"

"Seven-thirty sharp." Banks snatched up the coin and stood to leave. "Don't be late."

54

ELIJAH ARRIVED AT Prospect Street half an hour early and was rewarded with French toast, bacon, and coffee with Banks on the front porch.

"It's good," said Elijah.

"I lied about not being able to cook," said Banks. "I can cook French toast and grilled cheese sandwiches."

The fog was burning off with the early sun. Elijah wanted to get started on the driveway, but Banks was unusually talkative.

"The last time I was at church, your mother said something about a scholarship."

"Maybe," said Elijah.

"That's good, no? I bet lots of kids your age dream of going to Syracuse to play ball."

Elijah studied the sludge on the bottom of his ceramic mug, which reminded him of his mother and her Turkish coffee. He knew how she felt about a college scholarship to SU. It was a gift on par with winning the lottery. So how could he even consider turning it down? "I like the college part but not the basketball. I don't feel like playing anymore. I know that must sound crazy."

"Maybe. It looks like you were made for it," said Banks. "But it's no crime to *not* want to play ball."

"I think my mom would disagree," said Elijah. "In her world, passing on a scholarship is a major crime."

"She's a religious woman, right?" said Banks. "Just tell her, and then ask for her forgiveness. Isn't that how it works? By the way, you're almost done with the list. All that's left after the driveway is to do the gutters and then power wash the house and the garage. And you might as well mow the front lawn one last time."

"With or without the forty-five-pound plate on it?"

"Forty-five?" said Banks. "I'm thinking you're ready for a forty-five *and* a twenty-five. If you're feeling strong, that is."

IT TOOK ELIJAH the rest of the day to finish the driveway. He stopped for lunch, and again when Kerri pulled up in her red Fiat. As usual, she carried a book—*The Executioner's Song,* by Norman Mailer—and sat down cross-legged, close to where Elijah worked.

"You never called me," she said. "I didn't get to say how sorry I am about your friend."

"Thanks." He dropped to his knees and snugged the last paver into place. "I should have called, but I haven't felt like doing much."

"Except for working on the driveway," said Kerri.

"Right." He stood up and shook the sand off his T-shirt and jeans. "It's good for me to keep busy like this."

"I've been keeping busy, too. Working on that plan I never got to tell you about."

Elijah studied her, trying to figure out where this was going, and if he could allow himself to enjoy talking with a pretty girl. A part of him felt like it was too soon, that he should still be feeling sad and guilty. But another part of him imagined what Dylan would have said: *Dude, she's pretty. Talk to her!*

"I've got to put these tools away," said Elijah. "But I'm listening."

"How about we go somewhere?" Kerri closed her book and jumped to her feet. "I found a new coffee shop on Fremont. It's loud and anonymous, so no one will pay attention to what we're saying."

"I don't know." Elijah smiled his first smile since his friend's death. "That sounds a lot like a date, and you specifically told me you were unavailable. I think it's important for a person to stand by her word."

Kerri punched him in the arm. "It's definitely not a date. More like a strategy session."

Again, he imagined hearing Dylan's voice, encouraging him.

"Okay." Elijah started picking up tools and headed for the garage. "All my life I've been dreaming that a pretty girl would ask me out for a strategy session. But I've got some things to take care of first. Can it wait a couple of days?"

"Deal," said Kerri.

HE ARRIVED AT the bus stop at five. From a distance, he watched his former best friend sitting inside the kiosk, smoking a cigarette. Michael swiped his phone on, checked it, and then put it back into the pocket of his oversized, expensive jeans. He pinched the cigarette between the C of his thumb and first finger, dragging, and then breathing out. He looked experienced, even though Elijah had never seen him smoke.

"Hey," said Elijah, banging on the grimy plastic sheeting that made up one of the walls of the bus stop.

"Oh shit!" Michael turned around, eyes narrowed with alarm. "Damn, Elijah, don't do that, man."

"Who'd you think it was?"

"I don't know, man. That's why I freaked. I'm jumpy these days."

"It's just me. Since when do you smoke?"

"Since my life got filled with so much stress. Since I started feeling like I'm thirty-five years old."

"Maybe you can get into bars now, or buy beer."

"Yeah." Michael forced a laugh, but they were going through the motions, going about the business of friendship mechanically, without feeling. The bus rolled to a stop with a rush of air brakes;

the boys stepped in and found an empty row of seats in the far back.

"I don't know if I'm ready for this," said Elijah.

"Me neither," said Michael. "I ain't visited a grave before."

Elijah held a bouquet of plastic flowers and a small metal Mustang convertible. "I got this to leave on his headstone, but now it seems kind of stupid. You know he was always talking about getting a real one someday."

"It's cool." Michael held up a grocery bag. "I got him a *Playboy* and some X-Men comics."

"Keep the *Playboy*; it'll freak his mom out. Which X-Men?"

"The one with that hot girl he likes."

"The Scarlet Witch?"

"Yeah, her. She is pretty fine for a cartoon, but I wish I would have told him that when I had the chance."

"It's a good gift. He'd like that."

They got off at the Kensington stop and walked silently to the cemetery. The outer wall was cement topped, with wrought iron spires that formed an arch over the access road. They stood beneath it listening to the engine noise from the street, not sure what to do next.

"Are we supposed to go in?" asked Michael.

"I guess so. Dylan's mom gave me a map." He unfolded it and pointed at the *x* that marked their friend's site. They crunched along the gravel and down a small footpath. Elijah paused to read the first gravestones, which were made of marble and were very old.

"Look at this one—died in 1863," he said. "It says he fought in the Civil War."

"Yeah, it'd be cool if we were coming for something else," said Michael. "Like a school field trip or something. But this, for Dylan? It ain't right."

"No, it's not."

They were getting close; their pace slowed dramatically, as

though they could stave off the inevitable by drawing out the time it might take to get there. Michael clutched the grocery bag tightly against his chest. He approached the rectangle of earth that hadn't yet grown over with grass. "There's a little plaque there. How come there's no stone?"

"Because a stone takes weeks to make," said Elijah.

"Don't read it," said Michael.

"Why not?" asked Elijah.

"Because as soon as you do, then it's gonna be real and I gotta accept it. You know?"

Elijah nodded. "We have to read it, though. I think it's time."

"You read it to me."

"It says, 'Dylan James Buchanan. 1997 to 2014. Beloved son, brother, and friend.'" They took it in silently, and then got close enough to touch the letters and numbers that had been cut into the granite with some kind of a V-shaped bit.

"You know that he was the best of us, right?" said Elijah.

Michael dropped down on his knees in the freshly placed earth. He looked like he was someplace far away. "What?"

"I said he was better than both of us."

"I know it."

"I mean, he trusted us, and we were supposed to look out for him. We were supposed to keep him out of trouble."

After a time, when the silence became unbearable, Elijah set the flowers and Mustang next to the plaque. Michael took the comics out of the brown paper bag and placed them next to the flowers. His eyes were red-rimmed and swollen. "You know what I think?"

"What?" said Elijah.

Michael lay down on his back in the fresh dirt. "I think I'm ruined. I picked the wrong people; I should have picked you and Dylan. You guys were the good ones, not Money and them others."

Elijah moved a step closer. "You're not ruined."

"No, I'm serious." Tears and snot ran freely down the sides of Michael's face. "You should get as far away from me as you can, 'cause you ain't bad on the inside. You're still good. I can see it in you."

"You don't know what you're talking about," said Elijah.

But Michael was no longer listening. He sat up and smoothed the pages of the comics and rearranged the plastic flowers. He struggled to his knees, and then his feet. "I wanna leave this place."

THEY WALKED DOWN the path and back through the wrought iron archway. Michael's knees and the back of his pressed white shirt were stained with dirt, but he didn't seem to notice or care. On the way back they stopped at the Battlegrounds and sat quietly on the splintered bench. They observed the first signs of normalcy returning to the place—guys hanging out and talking trash, pickup games, even Jones spouting off his impressive-sounding bullshit under the live oak tree.

Elijah was the first to break the silence. "You know, I almost wish they'd shut this place down. So nobody could play here anymore."

"How come?" said Michael.

"Because I feel different inside. Like the part of me that used to come here and play ball with you and Dylan is gone. But this place doesn't care; it just goes on like it always did."

"What's the word for that—*indifferent?*"

"Yeah, that's it."

Michael took a deep breath and crossed his arms over his chest. "Maybe that's what happened to me. Maybe I got indifferent. That's why I don't care no more."

They walked past Antonio's, but neither felt like stopping for a slice. And later, outside Elijah's house, Michael stood stiffly, rubbing his face like a drunken man trying to wake himself up. "I'm gonna find out who did it, Elijah. I'm gonna find out who killed Dylan. You believe me?"

"I don't know if it matters anymore, Michael. He's dead."

"What do you mean it doesn't matter? It matters."

"I'm afraid no one cares." Elijah closed his eyes, trying to focus enough on the idea he'd thought but not put into words. "Nothing stops just because Dylan's dead. You know what I mean? He gets a little rectangle of land in the cemetery, and you'll keep on doing your business, whatever that is, and I'll move to Buffalo with my mom and finish high school there. We'll all just keep going, and I know that's how it's supposed to be and I don't have to like it, because that's how our world works. That's what I mean when I say it doesn't matter."

Elijah turned away and walked inside.

"GIVE ME A HAND WITH THESE?" Elijah's mother was struggling to get inside with a stack of cardboard boxes that had been folded flat and taped together.

He ran to the front door to help. "What are these for?"

"So we can start packing." She smiled when she said it, but didn't look him in the eye.

"But we're not moving for another month, right? You said the end of summer."

"I don't want to wait that long. *We're* not going to wait that long."

"Why not?"

"Because yesterday you and Michael went to visit your friend's grave. That's why. Do I need another reason? Elijah, he was shot in his back outside his home!"

He tried to say something, but she cut him off with a raised hand. "I don't own this house, and we're on a month-to-month lease, so we can leave whenever we want. There's really nothing holding us back, Elijah. I'll miss church and Pastor Fredericks, but he's already connected me with a new church in Buffalo. And you don't even seem interested in basketball anymore."

"I'm not. I want to be—because I want to go to college, and

I don't want to let Sam Lehigh and you down—but I don't want to play anymore. I'm sorry. I'll have to find another way to go to college."

"Elijah, I don't care about any of that right now."

"Maybe I can join the army, like Banks. Or work and save money. Maybe I can—"

"Elijah, come here, Son." She set the folded boxes on the counter and opened her arms. "Just let it go for now, and we'll figure it all out together. Okay?" She wrapped her arms around him and felt his tears trying to force their way out, through the protective layers he'd built up in the course of learning how to deal with all he'd been through so far. Some of them were things he hadn't yet told her about. "We've got two weeks to pack and get ready. After that, we'll start over again in Buffalo. It's going to be fine. You'll see."

"I thought he'd come, Mom," said Elijah.

"Who, Son? Who did you think would come?"

"Dad."

"Oh, Elijah."

"I thought if my team made it to the end of the tournament, to the championship, he'd come and watch me play. I thought I'd see him in the crowd, and he'd be proud of me. I don't know why I thought that, but I did. I said it over and over in my head until I believed it. That's how stupid I've been."

"Son."

"But he wasn't proud of me, Mom. He didn't come back."

"Let me tell you something about your father that I've never told you before," she said. "Maybe I should have. Maybe if I had, you wouldn't have spent so much time getting your hopes up, and then blaming yourself."

Elijah looked up, waiting to hear.

"When I met Will Thomas, your father, I knew he was a good enough man, but I didn't know how scared he was. All I saw was this big, strong, handsome black man who used to come into the restaurant where I worked as a waitress. Every day he'd wear a T-shirt with his tool belt slung over his shoulder, and I swear I felt dizzy on my feet whenever I looked at him. That's how handsome he was; it was the same for the other waitresses, who used to fight over setting his table."

"And you got it?" asked Elijah.

"No," she said. "I had the seats along the counter, where all the old men used to sit. Except, one day Will walked right past the hostess station and took a seat at the counter. He sat there every day for two weeks before he asked me out."

"And you said yes?"

"I sure did. And six months later I was married and pregnant, but Will Thomas was nowhere to be found."

"I thought you said he left when I was two?"

"That was the last time he left, but not the first. He'd go away for a week at a time on these construction teams. Jobs that were a hundred or so miles away."

She paused, remembering. "At first it was hard, but I got used to it. There was enough money, and there was you—you were a wonderful baby. But . . . the one-week jobs became two- and three-week jobs, and there wasn't as much money coming in. That was when I figured it out."

"Figured what out?"

"There was no out-of-town construction job."

"What do you mean?"

"He was still working around town, but living with another woman. Pretending to be far away. He made the whole thing up."

"Why?"

"That's what I wanted to know. I was twenty-two years old, Elijah, and with a baby. I went into the restaurant where I used to work, because I thought I might be able to pick up a few shifts and make some money. But when I got in there, guess who I saw, sitting at the counter talking to the next twenty-two-year-old waitress? That's right. William Thomas."

"Did he try to explain?"

"Yes, he did. And I was dumb enough to listen. That's why you've got a picture from when you were two, because I took him back."

"Still, it doesn't sound like he was afraid."

"Elijah, that man, your father, has started and walked out on several families. Whenever the responsibilities became real, he left. I found that out a little too late, I guess. I would feel sorry for myself, except that I got to keep you. So the name William Thomas doesn't make me angry or sad; it makes me feel grateful that I got to be your mother."

After a moment, Elijah said, "I've got half brothers and sisters?"

She nodded. "If you decide you want to find them, I'll help."

"Okay, I'll think about it," said Elijah. "But why didn't you tell me?"

"The truth? I guess I was hoping he'd come back, too. Which, I suppose, makes me the stupid one again."

ELIJAH FORGED AHEAD with Banks's list, which was as good a distraction as any. And there was the added benefit of avoiding Money. But as much as he enjoyed the power washer with its cooling back spray, he dreaded the awful weighted-down lawn mower, which Banks had specially prepared with a forty-five-pound plate and a twenty-five.

Banks watched from the front porch as Elijah fought with the ridiculous machine. Cigar in mouth, he offered no help other than the occasional disparaging remark. *Put your back into it. Come on, cream puff. You're better than that.*

Most of Elijah's efforts to get the impossible thing to move were of no use. In the end, it was a combination of willpower and brute force that coaxed it into motion. First, the rubber wheels rocked back and forth in their hard-packed, shallow ruts. Elijah felt the movement and pushed even harder, gritting his teeth, not caring if spit flew from his mouth and flecked his shirt and arms.

"You got it!" shouted Banks. "Keep pushing."

Veined muscles jumped beneath his skin, sneakers scraping the dirt for traction, and still he pushed harder.

"It's moving," said Banks. "Dig, dig, dig!"

Elijah's body poured sweat. His stomach tried to convulse from the superhuman effort, until, on the second-to-last pass, the push bar sheared in half. He tumbled to the grass, panting and heaving like a broken workhorse.

"Not half bad." Banks inspected him for injuries, grinning around his cigar. "Put this thing away and then meet me in the basement. I need some more help with my shadow box."

BANKS'S WOODSHOP WAS a model of organization. Every tool hung on the wall on its own peg, with a thick black outline to let him know if anything was missing. The surface of his bench was clean and freshly oiled, and the concrete floor was spotless. There was only one problem—Banks. In short, he had no clue what he was doing and was relying more and more on assistance from Elijah.

"I put a new blade on." Banks touched it to show him. "Like you said. It cuts better, but everything is still coming out wrong. The joints aren't square."

Elijah studied the defective pieces, and then the saw. "It's not the blade; you have to get the fence straight, like this." He took a tape measure and squared the fence to the blade, taking care to measure at both the front and back teeth. "Now try it."

Banks fired up the machine and ripped out new pieces. They checked the fit together.

"Good," said Banks. "Thanks."

"What was that last part?" Elijah shook his head. "I didn't quite hear you."

A faint grin. "I said thanks, but don't push it."

"You say that like it hurts."

"That's because it does." Banks laid the pieces out, and Elijah handed him a bottle of wood glue. "It's painful to be indebted to a smug kid. When's the big move?"

"Next week," said Elijah. "Just enough time to finish your project. Who knows? Maybe you'll get lucky and pull out a D."

"I'd be very happy to earn a D. Did you decide about playing basketball for the new school?"

Elijah shook his head. "The guy from Syracuse keeps calling. He wants to set up a visit."

"Wouldn't hurt to check the place out."

"I don't know. What if I don't play?"

"You don't owe them anything. Check it out."

"Yeah?"

"Sure. I would." Banks handed Elijah another plain white envelope. "Here's your pay, and there's a note from Kerri in it. She made me promise not to forget."

THE NOTE SAID to meet at the coffee shop at six o'clock. It also said no rain checks and that he'd better not stand her up. Elijah smiled as he read it, and then hustled home to grab a quick shower and a change of clothes.

His mother caught him on his way out the front door. "You just got home. Where could you possibly be going?"

"To meet a friend at the coffee shop."

"I see. And does this friend have a name?"

"She does."

"Well." His mother stood with her hands on her hips, smiling. "And did your other friend, Michael, find you?"

"No, why?"

"He came by. I told him you were at Mr. Banks's house. He was upset about something. Said he'd come back, that he had to talk to you."

"Okay," said Elijah. "I won't be out too late."

58

THE DATE, IF IT EVEN WAS ONE, didn't go as Elijah had expected. For starters, Kerri brought a dozen manila envelopes filled with her *research*. She spread the folders on a café table while Elijah ordered and waited for their cappuccinos.

"I can't wait to tell you," she said when he returned.

"Tell me what?" Elijah pushed a folder aside to make room for their drinks.

"Okay, so I know my father spilled the beans about being in Special Forces, but did he tell you he was an expert in unconventional warfare?"

"What?"

"Wikipedia says it's an attempt to achieve military victory through acquiescence, capitulation, or clandestine support for one side of an existing conflict. But really, it's destroying your enemy by using his strengths against him. Here's a cool example; it's not military, but it really happened." She opened one of the folders, which contained photocopies of an old Superman comic titled "Clan of the Fiery Cross."

"In the forties, this guy, Stetson Kennedy, wanted to stop the Ku Klux Klan, but everyone told him it was impossible. So he went undercover and learned the Klan's secrets. Then he approached the guys who wrote the Superman comics."

"You lost me. Comics?"

"They did a whole multi-episode thing about Superman fighting the Klan. The story revealed the Klan's secrets and made fun of the Klansmen. It worked so well that by the end of the series, Klan enrollment was down to almost nothing, and people were showing up at rallies just to mock them."

"That's true?"

"Yep."

"And that's unconventional warfare?"

"It's just an example. My father still can't tell me everything about the things *he* did. But the principles are the same: gather intelligence and find your enemy's weak point. Then—and this is the really cool part—you destroy him by turning his own strengths against him."

"And you're telling me this because . . ."

"Because we can do the same thing with Blood Street Nation. They can't be harder to take down than the Klan. The Klan killed thousands. Lynched people. Corrupted our own government."

"But why?"

"What do you mean why? Didn't they threaten you and your mom, and kill your friend? Aren't those good enough reasons?"

"For me they are, but not you. You're not involved. That's good. Aren't you leaving for college anyway?"

"Not for three more weeks. Listen, you don't have to worry about me, Elijah. It's sweet and all, but I'm nineteen, and I'm dead serious about this stuff."

"I know, but . . ."

"Hey, you took your team all the way in the tournament, right?"

He nodded, not sure of the connection or of how to slow her down.

"You had to be pretty focused on that goal to achieve it. That's how focused I am with this. You have basketball; I have this. I'm going to go to college to study forensics and criminology. When I'm done, I'm going to join the FBI. This is kind of like practice. Get it?"

"No."

Kerri continued, undeterred. "See these folders? I've worked out a whole plan. Just hear me out, okay?"

"Sure, but tell me this: do I have a part in this plan?"

"Of course." She beamed. "It's a great one, too. Lots of research involved, but you'll love it. Promise."

59

AT HOME, ELIJAH got to work researching the links and pdfs Kerri had given him. He read everything he could find on Banks's Special Forces unit, about which there was precious little. Apparently his division was so special that it didn't even have a name. Instead, there was a list of known conflicts and an even longer list of alleged ones. But he hit gold with a free pdf version of the *The U.S. Army/Marine Corps Counterinsurgency Field Manual,* a massive volume of explicitly detailed information on how to dismantle terrorist cells and enemy governments.

Elijah lay on the couch with his mother's laptop propped on his chest. He read for three hours straight, what he learned made his half-baked plan with the gun embarrassing. He'd had no clue what he was doing, and he thanked God he didn't have any blood on his hands. He didn't actually believe Kerri was going to take on and dismantle Blood Street Nation, but neither did he see the harm in playing along. Besides, it was interesting, and it was better than sitting back and doing nothing.

HIS MOTHER FOUND him asleep on the couch with the laptop still glowing. "What on earth are you reading?"

Elijah peeled his eyes open and took in his surroundings. "It's from Banks. An army thing. What time is it?"

"Eleven at night," she said. "Don't you hear that phone ringing? It's sounded off at least three times."

He dragged himself off the couch and picked up his cell without bothering to check the caller's identity. "Hello?"

"It's me, Michael." A heavy bass line pumped from a subwoofer in the background. There were voices, too.

"What's up?" Elijah thought about the dozen different meanings behind that simple question. How did he mean it? Not friendly, but not unfriendly, either. The way it was with people who used to be good friends but had grown apart. No, that wasn't true, either. *Complicated* was the way to put it.

"Listen," said Michael through the static of a weak signal, or maybe a hand cupped around the phone. "I think I found out who shot Dylan."

Instantly Elijah's heart began thumping its own dangerous bass line. "Who?"

"I can't talk here; it ain't safe."

"Where are you?"

Elijah heard street noise in the background. Someone cursing. Whatever was going on, it didn't feel right. Michael was in some kind of trouble. He just knew it.

"I'll call you tomorrow and tell you when we can meet." Michael sounded different, too, shaky and panicked.

"I'm working tomorrow. How about you say what you have to say right now? Tell me where you are."

A pause. The line went dead.

BEFORE GOING TO Banks's house in the morning, Elijah quickly covered the two blocks to Michael's house and banged on the door. He waited, and then knocked again. Just before giving up,

Michael's mother answered the door; her eyes were ringed with heavy bags, and she looked like she hadn't slept in days. From her fingers, a cigarette trailed smoke like a warning flare.

"Elijah." Her voice was as taut as a wire, and he guessed she'd been up all night. "Come on in."

"Hi, Mrs. Henderson." He stepped into the living room, covered in white pile carpet. Several pairs of Michael's sneakers were neatly lined up against the baseboard, like a collection. Above them, framed family pictures hung on the wall; the center picture showed him, Dylan, and Michael, all ten years old, at a swimming pool. The sun lit up beads of water on their skinny arms. They looked happy.

Elijah made sure to step on the welcome mat. "Is Michael here?"

"He told me he was spending the night at your house." She took a drag on the cigarette and closed her eyes for the briefest moment. "But I'm not surprised. He's been telling me all kinds of things, and only half of them true." She grabbed an ashtray off a nearby bookshelf, and almost dropped it.

"Do you know where he might be?" But even as he said it, he knew the answer.

"No." As she stabbed her cigarette into the tray, the weariness drained from her features and was replaced with fear. "He's in trouble, I know that. I'm afraid for him, Elijah. You'll tell me where he is, won't you?"

"I don't know where he is, Mrs. Henderson."

"But you'll find him, won't you? Please, find him and bring him home to me."

"I will, Mrs. Henderson."

She set the ashtray down and took his hands in hers. He could see in her eyes that she was close to tears. "Do you promise?"

"I promise," he said. But the world was too dangerous for promises like that. "Goodbye, Mrs. Henderson."

Thirty minutes later, Elijah checked the Battlegrounds, Antonio's, and even the courts behind the high school. But Michael was nowhere to be seen. Defeated, he moved on toward Banks's house, silently cursing Mrs. Henderson for having made him promise. He couldn't be responsible for anyone else. Look what had happened to Dylan after Elijah had said he would keep an eye on him. What could he do for Michael, who never listened to anyone? Michael, who was in deep with Blood Street Nation and claimed to know the identity of Dylan's shooter.

He stopped cold at the sound of his phone.

"Michael?"

"It's me," said a soft, feminine voice. "Kerri. How come you didn't come to work today? My dad was waiting."

"I'm actually on my way to your house."

"Okay, but hurry; there's something I've got to show you."

Elijah's mind boomeranged between Kerri's invitation and his strange, brief conversation with Michael, which carried the possibility of news about Dylan's killer. *There's something I've got to show you.* His head reeled with conflicting agendas, but in the end his lips moved and said the words "I'll be right over."

"Wait a second," said Kerri. "Did you think I meant . . ."

"What? No, I didn't."

"You did." Kerri laughed. "Admit it."

"Okay, I did, but so what? Can you blame me?"

"Listen, there's no time for flirting," she said. "I want to show you something on my computer. It's going to help us find Dylan's killer."

"Okay," said Elijah. "But first you've got to tell me, honestly, why are you so obsessed with this?"

"I'm not obsessed." She sounded mildly annoyed.

"You are. You've sent me at least two dozen articles on obscure principles of unconventional warfare. And you sound more interested in finding Dylan's killer than I am."

Kerri sighed. "Okay, but if I tell you, you've got to promise not to judge."

"I won't."

She took in a deep breath before getting started. "At first it was a way to get my father's attention. He thought it was cute that I knew more military history than he did. But as I got older, I learned two things. First, he wasn't an uncaring father; he was doing really important work. Dangerous work. It took everything he had."

"And the second thing?" asked Elijah.

"I learned that I have a good head for military and criminal justice stuff. It's like it is with you and basketball. It's my thing. Now get over here."

60

"COME IN, COME IN." Kerri threw the door open and led him to the kitchen; her laptop and manila folders were spread out on the table.

"Where's your father?" asked Elijah. "He's going to be pissed at me for being late."

"Downstairs working on his project," said Kerri. "And don't worry about being late; I made up a good excuse for you."

Elijah mimicked Banks's stern tone. "There is no such thing as a good excuse for being late."

"Right," she said, smiling. "But I lied and told him you had an appointment with the local army recruiter."

"What?"

"It was the best thing I could think of," she said. "Spur of the moment and all. He tried to be gruff about it, but I could tell he was impressed."

"You're scary," said Elijah. "Terrifying."

Kerri turned her laptop around to show the screen. "Look at this. It's so amazing, you won't believe it."

He bent down to see. "It's a map of the city. Congratulations. You discovered Google Maps."

"Very funny. Keep looking. See the blinking line?"

On the map, tiny red pinpoints marked out specific locations. A dotted blue line tracked the movements of someone or something.

"It's directions or a route. I don't know. Can you just tell me?"

"These dots are all the places where Money's been in the past two days. The blinking line is where he's going right now. Isn't this cool?"

"But how . . ."

"Okay, so I pushed the plan ahead a little bit. I'm sorry, but I think it's working."

Elijah stared. He remembered the coffee shop, Kerri turning over the small plastic square in her fingers, raving about how perfect it was. She'd called it elegant, because it was the easiest solution: cheap, reliable, and almost invisible. But still it had been an inert piece of technology; how had she gotten it to work? In the whole of Baltimore, she knew only her father and him.

"Okay. You told me that you first saw Money at the Battlegrounds, right? So I went there and talked to a few guys."

"Why?"

"To find Money. It was mostly a waste of time. None of the basketball players said they knew him. But there was this one guy who hung out by this old tree . . ."

"Jones."

"Right," said Kerri. "A little crazy, terrible dresser. Anyway, he told me where I could find Money, and so I went and found him. It was as simple as that."

Elijah started to pace the kitchen. "And what did you do when you found him?"

"Talked."

"Talked. About what? What could you possibly have to

talk to him about? Do you know who he is? Do you know what he did?"

"Relax, Elijah. That's, like, five questions." She grinned. "All I did is lean into his car window and make stupid conversation."

"What did you say?"

"I said, if someone new in town was going to throw a party and wanted to buy some weed, where would she go?"

Elijah paced and shook his head. "I can't believe you. Of all the people in the world to talk to, why him?"

"Because we need information, right? And it worked. He gave me his card. See? I dropped the chip into the little slot where the window goes—you know, between the two rubber seals—and now we've got all kinds of data. In two days we'll know all his routines, contacts, et cetera."

Elijah rubbed his temples and tried to calm himself. He'd never encountered anyone like Kerri before. She was always two steps ahead, and fearless! Worse, she was seriously beautiful, the kind that deepened the more he got to know her. They'd been arguing for twenty minutes, and he couldn't take his eyes off her, or get over the way she tucked her hair behind her ear, only to have it fall in her face seconds later. Other girls did the exact same thing, but with her it was different. Special. Or was he crazy?

Kerri smiled. "I think you're a little bit jealous."

"What? That's not it at all." Elijah sensed Banks lurking in the next room. He tried to keep his voice down "This guy's dangerous. He kills people!"

Banks walked barefoot into the kitchen, clinking ice cubes in an empty beer glass. "Who kills people?"

"No one, Daddy," said Kerri. "We're just talking."

"I heard half of what you were saying, you know. You two can't hide anything from me."

Kerri jumped up and kissed him on his stubbly cheek.

"Hypotheticals. You know I'm going to be studying criminal justice this year. I've created a hypothetical case to solve, involving local gang activity, and Elijah is helping me. Frankly, he's not very good at it." She made a frown at Elijah.

Banks touched the place of his kiss and smiled benignly. "You must really want me gone."

"As a matter of fact, we could use your help on this. Have a seat?"

"I'm retired, remember?" He eyed Elijah suspiciously. "You almost ready to get to work?"

"Yes, sir."

"When we're done, Daddy," said Kerri.

"Fine," said Banks. "I'll be sitting on the porch. You two be good."

AFTER THEY HEARD the front screen door slam shut, Kerri turned to Elijah and pointed a finger at him. "Don't underestimate me. I know how to take care of myself."

"He carries a gun!" said Elijah. "And you're hanging out with him?"

Kerri started laughing. "You can't even say his name, can you?"

Elijah slapped his hands over his head. "Are you always like this?"

"Always. Get used to it." And then, pointing at the laptop screen, she said, "Look, I see your point, but can we set that stuff aside for a moment?"

He slid his hands down to cover his eyes. "Honestly, I don't see how."

"Just remember our goal and set aside the human factor; that's how we'll get to the next step."

"The human factor?"

"Yeah, you know—people, relationships, feelings. They get in the way and cloud everyone's judgment."

"You're crazy," said Elijah

"Do me a favor, stop overreacting. Go play boot camp with my father, and I'll call you as soon as we get some useful data."

61

BANKS STOOD IN the backyard over a massive concrete boulder that must have weighed five hundred pounds. It consisted of several of the bigger driveway chunks, bound together with two crisscrossed lengths of welded chain. At the top of the chain was a heavy steel shackle; beside the boulder lay a hatchet-hammer combo, a four-by-four piece of timber, and the coil of black static rope he'd used to tear down the shed.

"What's this?" said Elijah, fearing yet another contrived task involving heavy things.

"Your next challenge," said Banks.

"I thought I was doing more yard work," said Elijah.

"This here is a problem that needs to be solved." Banks pulled out a cigar and ran it under his nose, inhaling deeply. "Remember when we ran into those thugs outside the diner?"

Elijah smiled. "Yes."

He lit the cigar and puffed it alive. "You asked if I could teach you some more of those things. That's what I'm doing. Now listen up, because I'm not going to repeat myself."

* * *

ELIJAH WALKED AROUND the boulder several times, trying to shift it even the slightest bit. He tugged on the chains. He whacked at it with the hammer, but the hardest blows produced hardly a crack. Next, he looped the rope several times around the nearest tree for mechanical advantage; the rope simply dug into the bark and locked up. Finally, he attempted to make a lever out of the timber, but it was woefully short.

Think. There's got to be a way.

"You giving up?" taunted Banks.

"No," said Elijah. It seemed impossible, which may have been the whole point. He'd seen a movie once where a genius kid had stopped a nuclear war by teaching an out-of-control supercomputer to understand the principle of futility. But he wasn't a genius, and nothing was at stake here, other than his own sense of pride. "Are there any rules?"

"Just one: using only the tools at hand, move the boulder twenty feet into the painted circle. I'll be in my workshop when you give up."

"Not giving up."

It took a full hour of thinking before the idea surfaced. Half an hour later, and he'd managed to chop the timber into four pieces of equal length, each one of which he sharpened into a big, wooden wedge.

ELIJAH STOOD AT the top of the basement steps looking into a cloud of sawdust and cigar smoke. "I'm done."

"Bullshit," said Banks from somewhere in the cloud. "Show me."

They surveyed the boulder, which had been reduced to a massive pile of chunks, the largest of which may have weighed in at fifteen pounds. Every piece, however, fit neatly within the painted circle.

"How in the hell . . ." Banks nudged one of the wedges with his boot.

"I learned it in earth science class," said Elijah. "Feather and wedge."

"Care to explain?"

"Before dynamite," said Elijah, "guys used to quarry stone using feathers and wedges."

"Skip the history lesson," said Banks. "Just tell me how you did it."

"Basically, they'd drill holes and then tap in long, thin wedges. The stone would split exactly how they wanted it to. I made some wedges and did the same thing."

"Okay," said Banks, "but you couldn't have drilled holes. No way."

"I didn't need to," said Elijah. "I found the weak spots and pounded until a crack formed. Then I put the tapered end of the wedge in the crack and pounded more. Three of the wedges split apart, but the last one held."

"That's . . ." Banks scratched his chin for several moments before finishing. "Damned creative. Good."

"How was I supposed to solve it?" asked Elijah.

"You weren't," said Banks. "It was supposed to be impossible."

"I don't understand," said Elijah.

"Futility." Banks crushed his cigar under a boot heel and turned toward the house. "That was the lesson."

62

THE FOLLOWING MORNING Elijah jogged to Banks's house, surprised at how much he was looking forward to the next chore/challenge. He surveyed the completed driveway, which he thought looked surprisingly good. The joints between the pavers were nice and tight, and the surface was smooth and uniform. There was only one irregularity, the absence of Banks's Jeep.

"Where's your father?" asked Elijah.

"The cigar store." Kerri grabbed him by the arm and pulled him inside. "I want to tell you something really important, and you have to promise not to freak out."

"I'm not going to freak out."

"What if it's something you don't want to hear?"

"About Dylan? You got more data from the GPS tracker?"

"No, it's not that. I pretended to go on a date with Money and got some really shocking intel."

"What?" said Elijah. "For a moment I thought you said you went on a date with Money, but that's too crazy to be true."

"That's right," said Kerri. "But it wasn't a real date."

"Describe what something that isn't a real date looks like," said Elijah. "Did you go for a ride in his stupid black Mercedes? I'll bet you did."

"We went for ice cream sundaes," said Kerri. "But it's not how it sounds. . . ."

"Ha." Elijah's phone pinged with a text message, but he was too enraged to notice.

"It was part of the plan."

"Because we needed intelligence, right?"

"Right. Don't you want to find out who killed Dylan and make sure they pay for it? I thought that was what you wanted. I thought that was the plan."

"That's *your* plan, Kerri. I don't have a plan. Every time I think I've got my feet under me, something happens and the ground shifts. So I guess you could say that my plan is to stand steady. That's it."

"Can we argue about this later? Can I tell you what I learned, and then you can get back to being mad at me?"

"Why him, Kerri? Of all the people in the world you could go out with, why Money?"

"Oh my God. You think I actually like him, don't you?"

"It sure looks like it. First you went and talked to him. And then you two had sundaes. What's next, a romantic weekend get-away?" He was grateful when his phone pinged again; this time he glanced at it and saw a text from Michael. It said, "Meet me at the Battlegrounds."

Kerri's face hardened. "Watch it."

But in a heartbeat, Elijah forgot the entirety of their argument. He pocketed his cell. "I've got to go."

"Wait," said Kerri. "Don't . . ."

But he was already gone, the front screen door slamming shut behind him.

63

AT THE BATTLEGROUNDS, Elijah sat on the familiar splintered bench and waited. There was no sign of Michael, but he could see Bull playing in a pickup game on one of the far courts. Elijah turned slightly away, hoping to stay off the big man's radar as long as possible; the last thing he needed was another fight.

"Come on, Michael," he muttered. "Where the hell are you?"

He thought about Mrs. Henderson's plea to bring her son home. And then there were Elijah's doubts. Truth be told, he wasn't sure he could trust Michael. He almost didn't recognize his friend anymore. Michael now smoked, and did *business* with Money, whatever *business* meant. Dealing drugs, and what else?

After a few more minutes, Jones spotted Elijah and came over to talk. He was wearing a yellow bicycling cap that said "Campagnolo," and a pair of old-school suede Pumas. You could say what you wanted about Jones—and lots of people did—but he had his own style. Elijah had to give him that.

"Hey, young blood," said Jones. It was his standard greeting to anyone under thirty.

"What's up, Jones?"

He pointed at the empty space on Elijah's bench. "You mind if I sit for a minute?"

"Go ahead. I'm waiting for Michael."

Jones sat down. "No worries. When your boy comes by, I'll hit it."

"What's up?" Elijah scanned the sidewalks leading into the Battlegrounds, but they were empty.

"Oh, you know." He took off his cap and finger-combed his hair. "A little business here and there."

Elijah watched the far court game where Bull had just committed an atrocious foul. His opponent was slow to get up, and limped to the take-back line.

"That's some ugly play," said Jones.

"Yes." Elijah looked around at the rest of the park and decided that it was all ugly—the game; the patchy grass littered with cigarette butts and candy wrappers; the bike frames stripped clean of their parts; and the padlocked, graffitied bathrooms. He had loved the place when Dylan was alive, but now . . . he couldn't stand it. He wondered if he'd ever play basketball again, and if things would feel any different in Buffalo. "Can I ask you something, Jones?"

"Still a free country," said Jones. "Go on and ask."

"Haven't you ever wanted to get out of here?"

"And do what?"

"I don't know. See the world. See how other people live."

"Oh, I see. I see. Well, I been out there, man. All over. California. Mexico. Oregon. Hell, I went to Asia once. You believe that?"

"Really?" Elijah didn't know if Jones was telling the truth or spouting more bullshit. That was the thing with him. You never knew what was fact or fiction.

"Yeah, they thought I was Kareem Abdul-Jabbar. All these little Japanese people coming up to me wanting to touch my Afro and have their pictures taken."

"Did you let them?"

"Why not? They was just curious. And curious is good, like the way you're asking this question about other ways to live. That tells me you're a thinking man. Thinking's good. Most people try not to think. You know that the human brain is designed to avoid thinking?"

"No."

"It's true. I listen to all these podcasts, and they had this Harvard neuro-something guy, and he said that thinking, as in real thinking—where you're solving problems and all—well, it takes lots of cognitive energy and it's the brain's job to conserve that energy, you feel me?"

Elijah narrowed his eyes, trying to puzzle it out.

"Basically," said Jones, "it's the brain's job to solve problems using as little brainpower as possible."

"That makes sense," said Elijah.

"But you didn't ask about that. You asked about seeing the world. I seen enough of it to know that nobody was going to hold a door open for old Jones. Or invite me to no country club. Man, I got a college degree! And after all that searching, all that looking around and checking things out, nothing was different. Or if it was, not different enough."

"So what did you do?"

"I come back here. I set out to work for myself, right under that oak tree."

"You like it?"

"Hell, yes. I keep it small so I can control every part of my business. If I can't see it with my own eyes, it ain't worth doing."

Elijah checked his watch one last time. "I have to get going, Jones. Good talking to you."

"Yeah, sure."

They stood up and shook hands; Jones's grip was crushing,

like a vise. Elijah tried to pull free, but the tall, thin man held firm. Elijah searched his eyes, which were filled with a burning, crazy intensity that made Elijah want to look away.

"I almost forgot," said Jones. "I have something of yours. Gimme a second and I'll get it."

Jones let go of Elijah's hand and whistled around two of his fingers. It was a long and shrill whistle, loud enough to reach the parking lot, where Money pulled his car into view and parked. It took him only a couple of minutes to walk over, carrying Jones's vintage eighties Adidas duffel bag.

"College Boy," Money said, shaking his head at Elijah, disappointed. "Not so smart after all."

"Go on and show him," said Jones.

Money took a big ziplock bag from the duffel and tossed it at Elijah's feet. "Have a look. Something special for you; I've been saving it."

Slowly Elijah bent over and retrieved the bag; it held a thin gold chain with a small basketball pendant. Dylan's necklace. The one he'd been so proud of. The one his father had bought him for his sixteenth birthday.

Jones beamed. "You putting it together, young blood? Yeah, I can see them gears turning. Good, good. Keep thinking."

Elijah unzipped the bag and removed the necklace. He understood now that it had been Jones all along. From the beginning. Watching him play ball and mess around with his friends. From the vantage point of his oak tree, Jones had been setting them up.

"It's you," said Elijah. "You're the boss."

"That's right." Jones slapped his long, skinny thighs. "I had some plans for you, boy. Good plans, too. I was going to back you to the Big Ten."

"What do you mean?"

"Finance you, man. Pave your way." His eyes grew wide with the excitement of an impending lecture. "Every top ballplayer's got a money trail behind him. Shoes. Food. Travel. A clean apartment without no parties or drama so you can actually get some rest. Tutors. Other stuff, too. Where do you think that money comes from? Things cost what they cost."

"I don't need your money," said Elijah.

"Everybody needs money. Don't matter now, though, 'cause you messed it up and got your friend killed. What was his name? Cody? Dustin?"

"Dylan." Elijah's mind raced to keep up, but Jones was too far ahead of him. "Why did you kill him?"

"Boy, I didn't kill nobody." Jones held out his palms for inspection. "Do my hands look like they dirty with stupid people's blood? Same goes for Money here. Him and me got us a ambitious young player who takes the trash out. You might even know him."

"Who? I know it's Money."

"Naw," said Jones. "I like names that mean exactly what they are. It's honest that way. Money deals with my money. Get it?"

The two men sat close together on the bench, laughing.

"The dude who takes out the trash goes by the name Assassin," said Money. "'Cause that's what *he* does."

Elijah fought back the urge to choke the answer out of them. How deep could he bury his thumbs in Money's windpipe before Jones pulled him off?

"You want to meet him?" asked Jones. "Be careful what you ask for now, boy."

"Yeah, I want to meet him."

"There." Jones jerked his thumb in the direction of the parking lot, where another figure emerged from the black Mercedes.

64

THE GLARE FROM the sun made it hard to see clearly, but Elijah would have recognized the swaggering walk of his big friend anywhere. "No. It can't be."

"It is." Jones cackled, clearly pleased with the turn of events.

"Assassin," said Money. "Also known as Michael Henderson."

"No." Elijah gripped Dylan's necklace inside a tight fist. "I don't believe it."

"You'd better believe it, boy!" Jones unzipped one of the end pockets of his duffel and pulled out a small black gun. He stood next to Michael and handed it to him. "'Cause you ain't observed my rules. Smart as you are, you thought you could do whatever you want and get away with it. You can't."

"What rules?" It seemed impossible that someone could shoot him in broad daylight in a public place, but two other dead boys proved otherwise. He wanted to look around for help, but he didn't dare take his eyes off the gun. He heard distant voices, though, and the throaty rumble of an engine revving somewhere in the parking lot. Money's black Mercedes? No, this was something bigger, like a truck or a muscle car.

"Tell him," said Jones.

Michael's voice wavered, but he forced the words out. "The

first rule is, if you screw up, somebody's got to bleed. Dylan already bled, so that one's covered."

"That's right," said Jones, nodding his head vigorously. "Second rule says, if you can't be trusted, you got to go. And you, College Boy, can't be trusted." He paused to suck his teeth in mock disgust. "So you gotta go now."

Michael pointed the gun at his oldest friend. His face was blank, emotionless; his green button-down shirt was crisp and perfect.

"You're supposed to be my best friend," said Elijah. "And you're going to kill me?"

"I got to," said Michael. "Boss says one of us got to go, and it ain't gonna be me. I'm sorry, man, but that's the way it is now."

"That's right." Jones bobbed his head in agreement.

"Come on, man." Elijah took a step toward Michael. He heard the engine sounds again, only louder. Money and Jones looked over their shoulders, trying to locate the source, but Elijah kept his eyes on the gun. He needed to stay in the moment, like in a game. He would focus and do whatever he needed to keep Michael talking and, more important, to keep him thinking. "You're still the same person. You're still my friend."

"I ain't." Michael held the gun steady, but beads of sweat were popping out on his forehead. "I killed Dylan, and now . . . I'm sorry, man, but this is who I am. This is me now."

"That's right," said Money, looking around him again, distracted. "You're the Assassin."

"Don't listen to him," said Elijah. "He doesn't know you. He doesn't know us. This isn't you, Michael."

Michael wiped at his eyes with his free hand. "It is, Elijah. I shot Dylan, and I shot Ray Shiver, too. Remember when I was telling you about crossing that line and how it gets a little easier each time? And then one day you wake up and you don't even recognize yourself no more?"

"Because you changed," said Jones.

Michael nodded.

Jones checked the screen of a cell phone tucked in his palm. "Time's up. Got any last words, boy?"

Elijah thought about all the people he would miss. His mother. Kerri. Even Banks, the grizzled Special Forces "accountant" who had once taken him for burgers and taught him his own brutally effective rule. What was it called? The law of the inexorables? He tried to remember, but there was a gun in his face, and also the engine whining somewhere in the distance. He needed to stop thinking and do something, but what?

"Yeah," said Elijah. "A couple."

"Let's hear 'em, then."

Elijah shifted his body slightly. He tried to appear relaxed, even though his nerves and muscles were strung as tight as wires. "Your rules are flawed. I've got one that's better. Want to hear it?"

"Your rule?" said Jones. "You ain't got a rule."

"Well, it's a law, really. It's called the law of inevitables." He spread his right thumb and forefinger, shaping his hand into a flat blade. His weapon.

"Never heard of it. You heard of it, Money? Assassin?"

Michael gave the slightest shake of his head. Elijah exhaled slowly once, twice, and then, without showing so much as the twitch of a muscle beforehand, he struck out with the inner plane of his hand, seeking the notch of cartilage just under the Adam's apple. There was a loud popping sound, followed by a terrible sucking of air. Michael dropped the gun into the cloud of dust at their feet. He clasped both of his hands over his throat. His eyes went wide with panic as he fought against the competing desires of breathing and clamping down on the awful pain.

Jones and Money circled, looking for the gun. Elijah stepped on it with his left foot and, at the same time, delivered a crushing blow with his right fist. It landed on Michael's cheek. Michael's head jerked backward from the blow, and he put up his fore-arms to block any further ones. Elijah felt consumed with rage; he ducked low and went to work on the body, throwing short, hard punches to the ribs and stomach. He drove his fists merci-lessly into Michael's soft middle until his enemy reeled backward and fell.

Elijah stood over Michael, the terrible engine sound filling his head. He wanted to look and find out what it was, but his foot had come off the gun. The weapon rested in plain sight between him and Michael. All Michael had to do was reach out; but he'd rolled onto his side, holding his ribs protectively. Elijah could see Jones and Money in his periphery, closing in.

Elijah made a stutter step to pick up the pistol, but Jones proved quicker. How could he be so fast? Elijah watched him grab it, his long fingers searching the metal casing for the safety, Money right beside him. Jones clicked the safety off.

"Time to go," said Jones.

Finally, after all of his efforts, Elijah was going to die.

He had thought that, in the end, he would be more frightened. But there was no fear, only the feeling that he'd done his best, that he'd tried to stand up for his friend, Dylan, who deserved better than to be shot in the back by a friend who had turned out to be a coward. A traitor. Elijah's thoughts were drowned out by the deafening sound—some kind of horn blasting over the grinding of a big engine working its way through its gears. What the hell was it? He looked up in time to see the vertical steel slats of a truck's front grill as it barreled straight toward him. How could there be a truck at the Battlegrounds? It made no sense at all, but there it was.

Instinctively Elijah fell back out of its path. He rolled in the dirt just as the vehicle, which he now recognized as a green Jeep Rubicon—Banks's green Jeep Rubicon?—took out the bench in an explosion of splintered wood and angle iron.

Jones threw up his arms and shouted something, but his words were drowned out by the spitting of oversized mud wheels fighting for purchase on the hard-packed dirt. A piercing squeal, more animal than human, rang out as the front end plowed into Jones's hip. His long, thin body flipped up and onto the hood and then, finally, crashed into the windshield. At the same time, the Jeep's door flung open and clipped Money in his back, sending him sprawling on his face just two feet from where Elijah lay. Only then did the truck stop.

65

ELIJAH PULLED HIMSELF up and surveyed the wreckage. Jones had slid off the hood and crumpled in the dirt near the Jeep's front fender. His right leg was bent at an impossible angle below the knee. His breath came in quick pants, and his face was covered with a film of sweat. Money was closer. His face had the shocked look of someone who has just had the wind knocked out of him—and gotten a few cracked ribs.

"Elijah." Banks killed the engine and slid down from the driver's seat. He looked at Elijah, running his eyes over him from head to toe, presumably checking for injuries. "You okay?"

Elijah nodded. "I think so. Yeah."

Banks smiled. "Good." He stalked across the dirt to where the gun lay. Picking it up, he emptied the chamber of its round and then popped the clip out of the grip. All of the pieces went into his back jeans pockets.

Money's breath finally returned to him, and he gasped. "Help. I think my ribs are busted."

"Shut up," said Jones. "You ain't hurt. Michael, get your fat ass up and help me."

In the distance, they could hear the warbling sound of police sirens.

"How did you know?" asked Elijah.

"I didn't," said Banks. "Kerri figured it out; I was just keeping an eye on her. You know those little GPS chips? Soon as I saw her with them, I put one in her car. Followed you two here."

"She's not here. It's just me."

Banks pointed across the street, toward Antonio's Pizzeria; her little red Fiat was parked out front. "I told her to stay put and call the cops. She can't come over here until they put cuffs on the bad guys." Banks patted down his pockets until he produced a cigar. He bit off the end and spit it in the general direction of Jones.

"It's probably killing her to wait," said Elijah.

"No doubt." He lit up and took a deep pull. "Where's the fat kid going?"

Elijah looked at the spot where Michael had been a moment ago; he'd pulled himself up and was in the process of limping away.

Banks shielded his eyes against the sun and scanned. "What's he doing?"

"I don't know."

They watched him skirting the outside of the fence by the basketball courts, still holding his stomach but jogging slowly. From the opposite direction came Bull, stalking his prey warily. Michael was busy looking over his shoulder; when he finally noticed the big man, it was too late. Bull backhanded Michael across the face so hard that it spun him around one hundred and eighty degrees. He followed with a vicious chokehold.

Elijah and Banks moved close enough to listen.

"I know you killed Ray." Bull loosened his grip. "Now say it."

Michael's mouth opened enough to speak. "I didn't—"

Bull squeezed, cutting off Michael's last words. "You killed him, and now I'm gonna kill you."

Elijah was certain that Bull would have kept his word if a trio of police cruisers hadn't encircled the courts. Two cops emerged from the first cruiser. They approached cautiously, guns drawn. "Hands up and back away."

"No," said Bull. "He killed my nephew."

Michael's eyes bugged even more.

"Easy there," said the lead cop. "What's your name?"

"I'll tell you my nephew's name," said Bull. "Ray Shiver. Shot up by this punk on Grider Street. That ring any bells for you all?"

The cops looked at each other. "Put your hands up and back away, sir. You have my word that we'll listen to your story."

"But right now," said the other cop, "you need to listen to us. And we need to see your hands. Now."

Bull didn't move, but neither did he continue cranking down on Michael's neck.

"The sooner you back off, the sooner we can sort this out."

IT TOOK MORE than an hour for the police to take statements and document the crime scene, all of which would go in the files connected to the Blood Street Nation case. Kerri joined Elijah and Banks; the three were made to tell their respective stories at least five times. It wasn't until later, after the cruisers and ambulances were loaded up, that Kerri threw an arm around her father and kissed his cheek. "You were amazing, Daddy. You came at just the right time."

Banks scowled. "You two could have gotten yourselves killed. You should have told me what was going on."

"I'm sorry." Elijah looked down at his feet, wondering how he was going to explain the day's events to his mother. It was almost unbelievable.

"Hell, don't be sorry." Banks examined the end of his cigar and relit it. "It was a tough situation; not many people could have done any better."

"You think so?" asked Elijah.

"Absolutely." Banks puffed intensely. "Which reminds me, I've got something for you in the Jeep."

"Go on." Kerri nudged Elijah; he followed Banks past a rusted drinking fountain and an overflowing garbage can.

The Jeep's front end was surrounded by the remains of the splintered bench and the broken glass from the shattered windshield. Elijah also noticed the dent in the driver's-side door from Money's back.

"Here." Banks opened the rear hatch and pulled off a canvas drop cloth; underneath it was a walnut shadow box, the one he'd been working on in his basement. The glass door had a large diagonal crack in it but was otherwise well crafted. The joints fit snugly, and the finish was deep and lustrous, the product of several hand-rubbed coats of linseed oil and wax.

"You finished it," said Elijah. "It looks great. I'm impressed."

"Look inside. There."

The display shelves were bare except for the top one, which held a single object. Elijah instantly recognized the shield and arrows, and the raised lettering that said "Special Forces Group."

"Is that . . ."

"You earned it. Go on."

Elijah opened the door and carefully handled the challenge coin. His chest and throat tightened, a clear warning that he was overwhelmed with emotion. "I don't know what to say."

"Don't say anything," said Banks. "People talk too damn much as it is. Take the whole box. I made two of them—one for you and one for me."

Banks took a step toward the garbage can and picked up a discarded ball with half its cover torn off. He spun it lightly in his hands. "You know I used to play a little."

"No kidding," said Elijah.

"Back in the day. Want to shoot a few? Unless you're still all done with basketball."

"Are you serious?" said Elijah.

"Of course I'm serious. I have no sense of humor." Banks stepped onto the court and tried to dribble the ball, which was nearly flat.

"Okay, then. Twenty-one, win by two," said Elijah. "You go first."

Banks's touch was surprisingly light; he nailed his first three shots, before banging the next one off the front of the rim.

Elijah dropped six straight before he was distracted by Kerri, who stood against the fence, watching them play.

"How about dinner?" she said. "All three of us."

Banks kicked the ball away. He found himself standing next to Elijah, his hand on the boy's shoulder as they watched Kerri approach.

"I don't know if it means anything to you," said Banks. "Or if I have the right to say it."

"Go ahead," said Elijah, the tight feeling returning.

"You did good, son." Banks gave a quick squeeze. "I'm proud of you."

Elijah tried to speak, but the words got caught up somewhere between his hopes and dreams, between his boyhood fantasies and the dark uncertain future of a seventeen-year-old. He wanted to let Banks know that he *did* have a right to say it, and it *did* mean something to him. Because he'd waited so long to hear those words, and the words had come to mean everything.

He wanted to say thank you, but he never got the chance. Because his eyes filled up with hot tears that began to spill over . . . with the sadness and fear and love and understanding of a boy who finally felt like he was home.

Wes's Acknowledgments

AS EVER, MY THANKS begins with my God, through whom all blessings flow. He guides everything I do. Shawn Goodman, it is a true joy working with you. One does not often find such a combination of talent and heart, and you have both in spades. To Beverly, Krista, and the entire Random House team, you helped to bring forth the idea and give it life. You are tremendous to work with. To Linda Loewenthal, thank you for always believing in me and my words. To my dear friend Seth Bodnar, you are more appreciated than you know. Your support and friendship are extraordinary. Thanks for your continued service! To my wife, Dawn, you motivate and inspire me. I could not be more grateful for you. Thank you for always standing by me and believing in me. To my kids, Mia and James, my world is better because of you. You give me point and direction. I could not be more in love. To Mama Win, thank you for being the matriarch and guide of our family. We all love you dearly. To my mom, words can never express what you mean to me. If I can be half the person and parent you are, I will be just fine. Nikki, Shani, Jamaar, Earl, and Rita, you are amazing in every way. Thank you for pushing me and inspiring me. To Uncle Howard, thank you for always motivating me. To my uncles Ralph, Bobby, Phil, and David and aunts Donna,

Pam, Evelyn, Dawn, Tawana, Michelle, and Valerie, THANK
YOU! You supported me before I knew how to support myself.
Bless you. To all of my younger nieces, nephews, and cousins—
Holley, Noelle, Earl, Bryce, Michael, Elijah, Tenai, Marcus, Erin,
Jaelin, Emory, Keston, Josi, Daniel, Anahi, Sebastain, Markie,
and Ava—you represent the best in all of us. I adore you and am
eternally proud of you. To my military brethren, thank you for the
motivation and foundation. Veteran is one of the most important
titles I own, and I could not be more proud of our fraternity. All
the Way! To all of my friends who support me and push me every
day, this book is a tribute to you. Thanks for everything you have
done for me and mean to me.

Shawn's Acknowledgments

THANKS TO MY WIFE, Jennifer Goodman, who is as lovely and
mysterious as when we first met. And thanks to Krista Vitola and
Beverly Horowitz at Delacorte Press and Seth Fishman at the
Gernert Company.

About the Authors

WES MOORE is an army combat veteran, a social entrepreneur, and the bestselling author of both *The Other Wes Moore* and *The Work*. He is also the host of *Beyond Belief* on the Oprah Winfrey Network and was executive producer and host of *Coming Back with Wes Moore*, which was broadcast by PBS.

Wes earned a Master of Letters in International Relations from Oxford University as a Rhodes Scholar. Upon graduation, he served as a paratrooper and captain in the U.S. Army, participating in a combat tour of duty in Afghanistan with the 82nd Airborne Division.

Wes founded and is CEO of BridgeEdU, an innovative educational platform that addresses the college completion and career placement crisis by providing freshmen with real-world internships and service learning opportunities. He lives in Baltimore with his wife and their daughter, Mia, and son, James.

SHAWN GOODMAN is a writer and high school psychologist. His experiences working with teens inspired both *Kindness for Weakness* and his first book, *Something Like Hope*, which won the Delacorte Press Prize for a First Young Adult Novel. Shawn lives in Ithaca, New York. Visit him at shawngoodmanbooks.com.